She felt him before she saw him.

The weakness and the strangeness of their situation must have made her more vulnerable than she'd thought, because when she finally turned and saw Dr. Parker Radcliff in the light, all she could think was, *Hello.*

Over the last month, she'd seen him more than she'd wanted to, catching glimpses of him as he'd gone from meeting to meeting, or when he'd swung by the front desk of the ER. She'd told herself she shouldn't even notice him, that he was nothing to her now. And she'd almost convinced herself it was the truth.

But now, seeing him up close in his street clothes with a good dose of five o'clock shadow, she was suddenly too aware of the strong angle of his jaw and the masculine hardness of his body.

Too aware that he'd just saved her life.

JESSICA ANDERSEN

DOCTOR'S ORDERS

HARLEQUIN®

TORONTO • NEW YORK • LONDON
AMSTERDAM • PARIS • SYDNEY • HAMBURG
STOCKHOLM • ATHENS • TOKYO • MILAN • MADRID
PRAGUE • WARSAW • BUDAPEST • AUCKLAND

To Denise Zaza and Allison Lyons for always
encouraging me to dig deeper.

ISBN-13: 978-0-373-88810-8
ISBN-10: 0-373-88810-4

DOCTOR'S ORDERS

ABOUT THE AUTHOR

Though she's tried out professions ranging from cleaning sea lion cages to cloning glaucoma genes, from patent law to training horses, Jessica is happiest when she's combining all these interests with her first love: writing romances. These days she's delighted to be writing full-time on a farm in rural Connecticut that she shares with a small menagerie and a hero named Brian. She hopes you'll visit her at www.JessicaAndersen.com for info on upcoming books, contests and to say "hi!"

Books by Jessica Andersen

HARLEQUIN INTRIGUE

*Bear Claw Creek Crime Lab

CAST OF CHARACTERS

Dr. Amanda (Mandy) Sparks—Four years ago she left Boston General with her heart in pieces. Now she's back and ready to prove herself. But when a killer sets his sights on her, can she turn to the man she once loved for help?

Dr. Parker Radcliff—Running Boston General's ER and consulting for the police force leaves Parker with little patience for emotions and no time for drama—until Mandy turns his world upside down again by getting mixed up in a dangerous case.

James Stankowski—The young police detective is Parker's only close ally. Can their friendship survive betrayal?

Anabella "Cutthroat" Cuthbert—The CEO of Boston's powerful UniVax Pharmaceuticals knows more than she's saying about the strange deaths occurring near Boston General.

Jeremy Deighton—This young, enthusiastic politician is looking to clean up the streets of Boston. How far will he go to succeed?

Paul Durst—This brilliant scientist is on the verge of a huge breakthrough…if he doesn't have a breakdown first.

Chapter One

"I'm sorry, Doctor, but Ms. Dulbecco died early this morning." On the phone, the nurse's voice softened. "Did you know her personally?"

Mandy Sparks gripped the handset tightly and turned her back on the chaos of the Emergency Services Department, so her coworkers—or one co-worker in particular—wouldn't see how badly the news had upset her. She looked down, and her long blond hair fell forward past her face, forming another barrier between her and the rest of Boston General. "I didn't know her well. She was a patient, that's all."

But to Mandy there was no "that's all" about it. As far as she was concerned, every case was special, every injury or illness a personal battle.

"She went peacefully," the nurse offered, as though that made a difference. And in a way, it did. Mandy hadn't been able to pinpoint the cause of Irene Dulbecco's pain, but she'd been able to make the forty-something mother of two more comfortable. She'd gotten Irene stabilized, and had sent her upstairs to the Urgent Care Department, where her husband and kids could visit more easily. Then, Mandy had gone home and crashed for six hours of badly needed sleep.

Logically she knew the staff members in Urgent Care were the best at what they did, but now she wondered if things would've gone differently if she'd stayed.

"If there's nothing else, Doctor…" the nurse said, drawing out the last word to indicate that it was time for her to move on to the next call.

It wasn't just her, either. The prevailing motto at BoGen these days seemed to be "move 'em in and push 'em out, and don't get emotionally attached," which Mandy found more than a little disturbing. Or maybe she was painting everyone else with a brush that belonged strictly to the department head, Parker Radcliff.

As far as she was concerned, Radcliff pretty much embodied the word *disturbing*.

"That's all," Mandy finally said into the phone. "Thanks for—" She broke off when the nurse disconnected before she'd finished, but kept the phone pressed to her ear for a moment longer, in order to buy herself some time to regroup.

I shouldn't have come back here, she thought, closing her eyes and pinching the bridge of her nose in an effort to delay the incipient headache. *I should've taken the job in Michigan.*

Unfortunately the smaller hospital in Ann Arbor had lacked the clout of Boston General, and Mandy needed at least another eighteen months of top-flight E.R. experience and a solid recommendation if she wanted a shot at winning next year's Meade Fellowship. With good E.R. openings in short supply, she'd been very lucky that her previous employment at BoGen had automatically moved her ahead of the other applicants.

Now, though, barely a month into her second stint at the hospital, she was starting to think she'd made a big mistake.

"Are you going to stand there listening to the dial tone all morning, Dr. Sparks?" Radcliff's voice said unexpectedly from directly behind her, interrupting her thoughts with the sarcasm he seemed to save just for her. "Or were you planning on seeing patients at some point today?"

Mandy stiffened, but forced herself not to stammer and retreat. Instead she took a deep breath, tossed her hair back from her face and turned toward the man she'd once—in a bout of youth and stupidity—thought she loved.

Radcliff's wavy, dark brown hair was tipped with silver at his temples, and faint creases fanned out from his dark blue eyes. Those small signs of mortality should've made him seem approachable, but the square set of his jaw and the coolness in his eyes formed an impenetrable barrier. He wore a crisp white lab coat, its breast pocket embroidered not with his name or title, but with two words: The Boss.

On any other man it might've been a joke.

On Radcliff, it was simple fact.

Four years ago, she'd been a lowly resident and he'd been the head attending, and ten years her senior. Now he ran the entire E.R., and spent more time on paperwork than medicine, which was lucky for her, because it had allowed her to avoid him since her return to BoGen. In turn, he'd limited their contact to snippy memos about increasing her patient turnover and keeping expensive tests to a minimum. On the few instances they'd been forced to interact face-to-face, they'd both made sure they were surrounded by a crowd of other staffers.

Until now.

Mandy's heart picked up a beat. "I was discussing a patient with Urgent Care. I saw her yesterday, and her symptoms didn't make sense to me. She passed away last night."

Radcliff glanced at his watch, sounding almost bored when he said, "She didn't die on your watch, which makes her Urgent Care's problem, not yours. And your shift started ten minutes ago."

Mandy couldn't believe he could be so callous about a patient's death. Sure, she'd heard the rumors that he'd only gotten colder over the past few years, but—

But nothing, her rational self interjected.

Don't think you know him now because you had a fling.

Knowing that little voice inside her was right, darn it, she said, "Sorry. I'll skip one of my breaks or make up the time after my shift."

Whether she liked it or not, she needed Radcliff on her side when it came time for recommendation letters. Dr. Stewart Royal, chairman of the Meade Foundation, had warned her that the competition would be fierce. She was determined to win the all expenses paid year abroad, though. She'd dearly love to get her hands on the funding and support, which she'd use to travel to Shanghai and study traditional Chinese medicine—TCM—with the master of the art, Dr. Li Wong.

Rumor had it the foundation was getting ready to award this year's Meade Fellowship, but she held out little hope for her application. She needed another year of solid experience in her field of E.R. medicine, and a glowing recommendation from a heavy hitter like Parker Radcliff.

Which meant no picking fights with the boss, no matter how much his policies irritated her. No matter how much *he* irritated her.

He stared at her for a long moment, his eyes shadowed with suspicion, as if thinking she'd forget about making up the ten minutes the moment she was out of his range. Then, apparently deciding she was sincere, he nodded sharply. "See that you do. And stop bothering Urgent Care. They have more important things to do than make you feel better about losing a patient."

"I wasn't bothering anyone. I—" Mandy snapped her mouth shut on the protest, but it was already too late.

"Yes, you were." He leaned in and reached for her, and for a mad, crazy second her heart thudded against her ribs at the thought that he was going to kiss her. Instead he plucked the phone handset from her fingers and hung it up with a decisive click. "Let it go."

She told herself to nod and scram, but the rebellious part of her, the one that constantly courted trouble even when she was trying to behave, had her muttering under her breath, "You can tell me not to call, but you can't keep me from caring."

The words came out far louder than she'd intended. They hung in the air between them, recalling the night four years earlier, when she'd hunted him down in the doctor's lounge at the end of a double shift to tell him she loved him, only to find that he wasn't just on a different relationship page from her, but he'd been reading from an entirely different book, one entitled, *Ten Steps To Recovering From Divorce.*

Step one, apparently, was to have a no-strings affair with someone the complete opposite of his ex-wife. Mandy, ten years younger, with California beach bunny looks and an easy, generous nature, had apparently fit the bill perfectly. Unfortunately for her, Radcliff hadn't thought to share the plan; he'd just assumed they'd both been in it for some good times and no regrets.

He'd been wrong.

For a moment she thought he was going to say something about that time, that he was finally going to acknowledge their history, if only obliquely.

Instead he stepped away from her and his voice chilled to glacial. "I may not be able to keep you from becoming unnecessarily involved with your patients, but I can and do expect efficiency from my staff. Have you looked out in the waiting area? How about the curtains or the exam rooms? They're all full of patients, *Dr.* Sparks." He paused, then said, "Don't you dare lecture me on caring unless you're out there dealing with patients, and if you can't do that, then start looking for another job. I won't allow you to disrupt my E.R." The words *not again* hovered between them, unspoken.

Temper sharpened Mandy's tone. "Then why did you hire me? You know how I practice medicine, and how my 'touchy-feely'—" she emphasized his long-ago sneer by sketching quote marks in the air "—methods drive you nuts. Surely you didn't think I'd changed." She paused. "You must've recognized my name when you saw the application." *Or did you forget me the moment I was gone?*

And the hell of it was, the answer mattered to her when it absolutely, positively shouldn't.

His expression flattened. "I think we both know it wasn't my decision to hire you." His lips twisted into a smile, though his dark blue eyes held no humor. "I guess you outgrew your vow to make it without your father's help."

"What does my father—" Mandy broke off when it suddenly made all too much sense. "Oh," she grated through clenched teeth. "I see." Damn him.

Part of her irritation redirected itself to a gut-deep frustration that hadn't changed over the years. She wasn't sure what piece of "stay out of my business and don't you dare call in any favors" her father hadn't understood, but she probably shouldn't have been surprised. Dr. David Sparks, plastic surgeon to half of Hollywood, had always possessed very selective hearing when it came to his only daughter. More tellingly, he was occasional golf buddies with three members of Boston General's board of directors.

He might not have any pull with the Meade Foundation, but he definitely carried some clout at BoGen.

Radcliff shrugged. "Doesn't matter to me whether you knew about your father's involvement or not. The bottom line is that I'm stuck with you for the next year, and then I'll be 'strongly encouraged'—" now it was his turn to emphasize the words with finger quotes "—to give you a glowing recommendation." He looked down at her for a long moment before he grimaced and dropped his voice to almost a conspiratorial whisper, "Look, I know you probably hate me for what happened between us, and maybe you're right. I could've—*should've*—handled things better. But you're the one who ran."

Because you broke my heart, you bastard, she thought, but aloud, she said simply, "I'm back."

He accepted the nonanswer with a nod, voice turning brisk. "We're both adults, so I'd like to think we can manage to get along for the next year. But that's going to mean you getting something straight—I don't care what you do in your spare time, but when you're on my clock, you're working, and that doesn't mean snuggling down for a series of bedside chats, or prescribing herbs and self-reflection instead of painkillers and blood pressure meds."

Mandy gritted her teeth. He wasn't the first to sneer at her use of non-Western medicine in a U.S. hospital setting, but his derision cut.

Unfortunately he also had a point. They needed to find a way to get along. "What exactly do you want from me?"

"I need you to process your patients faster. Do the basics. If you think there's something more complicated going on, come to me or one of the other senior staff members *before* you order a nonstandard test, or even better, turf the case to another department." He paused. "We're the front line of medicine, not a long-term hospice. Our motto is triage, then treat what you can and ship out the rest. Let the family members, the interns and the volunteers waste time holding hands. The doctors have more important things to do."

Which was just crap as far as Mandy was concerned. Emergency Services was where the patients needed the most reassurance, not the least, and the doctors were *exactly* the ones who needed to give that comfort.

"We'll have to agree to disagree on that one," she said, trying to match the coolness in his voice. "But I'll work on increasing my turnover rate."

"Fair enough." He gestured for her to get to work, but when she turned away and headed down the short hallway to the main desk, he called, "And, Mandy?"

Hating the shimmer that worked its way through her body at the sound of his voice saying her name, she paused and looked back. "Yes?"

"I want you to forget about Irene Dulbecco's death. Leave it alone and move on."

Mandy grimaced but said nothing as she turned and strode away from him, knowing she was better off retreating than arguing.

She was halfway to the front desk before she stopped dead and spun back around. "How did you know the patient's name was—"

He was gone.

PARKER STRODE OUT of the E.R., grimly aware of staffers ducking out of the line of fire as he passed. Good call on their parts, because he was in a mood.

When he reached the Atrium at the main hospital entrance, where the lack of sensitive medical equipment and the bustle and foot traffic meant he could use his cell without being overheard, he dragged out his phone.

Ducking into an alcove filled with potted plants, he dialed Stankowski's number. The moment the phone clicked live, he skipped the pleasantries and said, "One of my doctors is curious about the Dulbecco case."

Granted, Mandy had only just learned of her patient's death, but unless she'd changed drastically over the past four years—and he didn't think she had—her next step would be to check the test results and look for similar cases, which would raise some serious red flags.

"Tell her to leave it alone," Stankowski said in his trademark laid-back fashion, which camouflaged the fact that the young homicide detective had a hell of a sharp mind.

"I tried." Parker grimaced. "Trust me, that won't get very far. Mandy—Dr. Sparks is a pit bull on this sort of thing. Add in the fact that Dulbecco had a husband and two kids under the age of five—upping the sympathy factor—and she's not going to give it up easily. Either I figure out how to distract her, or we're going to have a problem."

There was a pause, and a note of speculation entered Stank's voice. "Mandy, huh? Is she cute? Maybe I could distract her."

"She's—" Parker broke off, surprised by the quick punch of anger that hit him in the gut at the thought of Stank getting anywhere near her. "She's not your type."

Actually, the long-legged, willowy California blonde was exactly the sort of type Stankowski gravitated toward—gorgeous, stacked and smart. She was also Stank's age, both of them in their early thirties, and they'd look good together, like they'd just stepped from the cover of a magazine devoted to young, upwardly mobile professionals who played extreme sports on their days off.

There was no way in hell it was happening, though. Not over Parker's dead body.

Four years earlier, fresh out of his divorce, he'd gotten involved with Mandy even though she'd been so wrong for him it had been laughable. He'd figured they could have some good times while it lasted, which had only proved his ex-wife's point—he didn't understand women, or their emotions. He hadn't realized Mandy thought they were in love until it was far too late, and he'd dealt with the guilt by being harsher than necessary.

"I get it," Stank said, a new note entering his voice. "She's *your* type. Interesting. I was starting to wonder if you even had a type."

"She's nobody's type," Parker snapped.

"So if you're not going to let me distract her, what do you suggest we do?" Stank asked.

Parker muttered a curse. "We need to move faster."

"No kidding." Stank paused, no doubt waiting for Parker to come up with a bright idea. When none were forthcoming, he sighed heavily. "Look, I think I might be onto something at this end. Just keep your doctor away from Dulbecco's case for the next few days, and we might be able to finish this thing for good."

"That'd be a relief," Parker said. "Thanks." But as he hung up, he wasn't feeling particularly relieved because Stank was right—there was no way he could see to get around it.

In order to keep Mandy out of trouble, he was going to have to do something he'd been avoiding for the past month.

He was going to have to spend time with her.

MANDY DID HER BEST to keep her mind off Irene Dulbecco's case during her shift. Her patients helped, providing the variety that was one of the biggest draws of E.R.

medicine. Against the standard backdrop of sniffles and sexually transmitted diseases, sprains and lacerations, she dealt with one toy car-up-the-nose, two MVAs—motor vehicle accidents—that she sent straight up to surgery, and a pregnant teen whose only ailment was a serious attack of nerves.

Though she normally would have spent time with the girl, Mandy knew Radcliff was watching her turnover figures, so she handed the mother-to-be over to a social worker and sent a quick prayer that everything would work out for the best.

Finally, exhausted from a single shift that had felt like an eternity, Mandy signed herself off the board and headed for the staff lounge, which was a comfortable room with a TV, kitchenette and couches, along with a row of lockers where staff members kept their street clothes and other personal effects.

Her spirits lifted when she saw her good friend, Kim Abernathy, sprawled on one of the couches in the main room. The petite brunette was wearing street clothes, indicating that she'd finished her shift upstairs in the Neonatal ICU.

Kim had her head propped up with a pillow, and her eyes were closed, and for a moment, Mandy thought she was fast asleep. Then the corners of Kim's mouth turned up. Without opening her eyes, she said, "Hey. You're late."

Mandy crossed to her locker, already shucking out of her scrubs. "Did we have plans?"

"Try checking your cell phone every now and then. The Wannabes are getting together down at Jillian's. They're expecting us."

Which probably meant Kim had set up the party in the first place. She'd always been the glue holding together the dozen or so premed students who'd met in college and had stayed friends in the years since. Members of the gang had come and gone over the years as relationships and jobs changed, but the spirit had remained the same. It was a group of up-and-comers who wanted to be so many things—doctors, researchers, professors, successes…some had made it big right out of school, others hadn't yet found their stride.

Mandy figured she fell somewhere in the

middle. She'd met some of her goals, like finishing med school and separating herself—mostly, anyway—from her father's influence. Other plans were in the works, like the fellowship. Still others, like finding love and starting a family, seemed further away each year.

At the thought of love and marriage, Radcliff's image popped into her head, causing her to mutter a curse as she dialed the combination to her locker and pulled out her jeans and a sweater.

"Problem?" Kim asked, opening an eye to look over at her.

"No. Well, yes." Mandy paused on her way to the changing area, her mind switching gears to the other thing that was weighing heavily. "One of my patients died last night. She had a husband, and two little kids, and yes, I know that shouldn't make her any more or less important, but…." She trailed off, then shrugged. "Sometimes it's just not fair."

It didn't take a psych specialist to point out the parallels between Irene and Mandy's own mother—both women in their early forties, both women struck down suddenly, leaving a family behind.

But while Mandy's mother had been murdered in a home invasion gone wrong, Irene had died of a disease. But what one? She'd been healthy aside from the pain, which had sprung up suddenly out of nowhere. Mandy's examination had turned up little more than a few bruises and a patch of healing road burn the patient said had come from having been mugged a few days earlier. None of it had explained the debilitating pain, or her death.

"Come on," Kim said. "I prescribe bar food and some Wannabe love. It might not fix everything, but you'll feel better. I guarantee it."

"You're probably right." Telling herself she was overtired and feeling vulnerable, that was all, Mandy changed into her street clothes and pulled on a heavy parka, hat and gloves as protection against the fierce New England winter.

She and Mandy left the E.R. together and crossed the main Atrium, with its soaring ceiling, central fountain and nearly deserted coffee shop, and then pushed through the revolving doors to Washington Street.

Outside, Mandy squinted against a sharp

slice of wind, wishing she'd worn another layer. When Kim turned toward the nearby MBTA stop, though, Mandy paused. She waved for her friend to keep going. "You head on over. I'm going to take a quick detour."

Kim narrowed her almond-shaped eyes suspiciously. "Where to? You're not trying to get out of having fun with the Wannabes, are you?"

"No, I just—" Mandy broke off, not really sure where the impulse had come from, or what she hoped to find. "I need to check something out. You go ahead and I'll catch up. I won't be long. Promise."

Kim muttered a good-natured insult under her breath, but headed for the T station while Mandy hung a right and crossed Kneeland Street, headed for Chinatown.

It was nearly 10:00 p.m. and no moon was visible in the winter sky, but she felt safe enough. There were plenty of streetlights and passing cars, and her destination was at the edge of the Patriot District, an upscale historical neighborhood that had little in the way of serious crime.

"Strange place for a mugging," she said to herself as she crossed the main street, headed for the alley where Irene Dulbecco had said she'd been attacked.

Mandy wasn't even sure what she was looking for—a dead rat, maybe, or a spore growth that shouldn't have been there.

Which just goes to show you've been watching too many medical detective shows lately, she thought as she stopped in front of the intersection Irene had described. It wasn't a street, so much as an alley between two tall brick buildings, creating a space of dark shadows that formed a stark contrast to the well-lit main street.

When nerves shivered down her spine, Mandy fumbled in her purse for her overloaded key ring, which held a miniature flashlight and a tiny can of pepper spray. She unclipped the pepper spray so she could hold it in one hand while using the flashlight with the other.

Feeling a little braver now that she was armed and semidangerous, she moved into the shadowed alley with only a slight quiver of fear, a faint sense that maybe this wasn't the best idea she'd ever had.

Splashes of light reflected in from the main road, enough for her to pick out the general shapes of Dumpsters and darkened doorways on either side of the narrow space.

"Let's see what we have here," she said quietly, clicking on her tiny flashlight and aiming the weak beam toward one of the Dumpsters, where a puddle of something had frozen to a hard slick in the winter air.

Thinking for a second that it looked like blood, she stepped closer and crouched down to investigate. As she did so, her flashlight beam caught a glint of something caught behind the wheel of the massive Dumpster. Feeling partly foolish, partly adventurous, she wiggled the thing free and came up with a flat disk that looked like a CD only smaller.

When she shined her light on the minidisk, she saw that it was labeled "ID."

Excitement worked its way through her. The letters could stand for Irene Dulbecco.

"Then again they might not," she muttered under her breath. She flipped the disk over, saw that there was a long scratch on the opposite side and shrugged before she pocketed the disk and straightened away from the Dumpster. "Let's see if there's anything else."

She squinted and swept the light from side to side, then focused the beam over into the far corner. The light was too weak to be much good, and she took two steps further into the alley.

A heavy blow hit her from behind without warning, driving her onto her hands and knees.

She screamed as she hit, heart locking on sudden terror. The key ring flew from her hand and skidded away as she twisted, rolling to her back just in time to see the darkened silhouette of a man leaning over her, holding something that glinted in the faint streetlights. For a second, she thought it was a gun. Then he shifted, and she saw that it wasn't a weapon.

It was a syringe.

Chapter Two

Mandy screamed and tried to roll away, but her attacker grabbed her jacket with his free hand and pinned her arms by holding onto both of her sleeves at once. She thrashed wildly as he kneeled partway across her, forcing her torso flat against the unyielding pavement.

Panic poured through her, and adrenaline gave her struggles renewed strength, but not enough to budge the man. He leaned down, and as he did, a shaft of light reflected in from the main street, giving her a glimpse of his face.

She got the impression of bitter gray eyes hidden within the hood of a heavy black sweatshirt, and saw lighter material covering his nose and mouth. Then he shifted his weight, pinning her fully with his legs so he could grab her upper arm and hold it steady.

Without a word, he swung the syringe sharply downward, plunging the needle through her parka, but missing her arm.

Mandy screamed as her attacker cursed and withdrew the needle, then aimed it at the meat of her arm. Just as the syringe descended a second time, a dark blur erupted from the shadows and slammed into him, jolting him off to one side.

She lay dazed for a moment, hearing grunts and the sounds of a struggle. Then a familiar voice snapped, "For the love of— Run!"

Radcliff? The shock of hearing—and recognizing—his voice sent a new burst of adrenaline through Mandy's system. Before she was even aware of moving, she'd scrambled to her feet and staggered back several paces. Then she stood, swaying, while the world spun around her.

In the dimness, she could make out the shapes of two men squared off opposite each other. The stranger wore a hooded sweatshirt and a light-colored mask beneath, along with what looked—oddly enough—like surgical gloves. Radcliff, on the other hand, wore dark jeans and a heavy leather jacket, and had a knit cap pulled over his ears.

The oddness of seeing him in street clothes rather than a lab coat created a disconnect in Mandy's brain, one that had her hesitating for a second. Then the hooded man growled something and lunged at Parker, swinging the syringe in a deadly arc.

Mandy screamed, "No!"

"Get out of here!" Radcliff bellowed. He ducked low and caught his assailant in the gut with his shoulder, folding the guy and deflecting his aim. Then he twisted and side-stepped, and grabbed the other man's wrist, fighting for control of the syringe.

Mandy wavered for a second, poised between running away from the fight and running toward it. Radcliff had ordered her to go, but as she watched, she saw his braced arm give under the other man's weight, saw the syringe drop a few inches closer to its target.

Don't be a fool, the cautious side of her inner self said. *Go get help. Call nine-one-one.*

But her cell was in her purse, which lay on the pavement just behind the combatants. There was no way she could reach it, no way she could get to her phone, and by the time she found help it might be too late.

Before she was aware of making the decision, the other side of her inner self—the one that was always making mistakes and getting her into trouble—had her launching into action. She lunged, not for the fight, but for the nearby Dumpster. Stretching her arm beneath it, she felt around in the frozen clutter, grimacing until her fingers found the tiny bottle of pepper spray. Heart pounding, she scooped it up and scrambled to her feet.

As she turned toward the combatants, Radcliff gave a low, bitter curse. The syringe hovered bare inches above his throat.

Before she could talk herself out of the mad plan, Mandy flipped the tiny safety off the spray and lunged, aiming the jet full in the other man's face, above what she now saw was a surgical mask to match the gloves.

The stranger looked at her, his pale eyes locking on hers for a split second as the spray triggered.

At the last possible moment, the hooded man stepped back, relaxed his grip and yanked the syringe away. Radcliff staggered forward, twisting as he fell under his own momentum.

"Watch out!" Mandy cried as he side-stepped and righted himself right into the cloud of pepper spray.

Radcliff howled and reflexively grabbed for his face before redirecting and lunging for his opponent once again, but it was already too late. The masked and gloved man spun away, bent down to grab Mandy's fallen purse and keys and bolted from the alley.

Streetlights silhouetted him briefly against the mouth of the alley as he skidded, hooked a right and disappeared.

Swearing, Radcliff lunged in pursuit, caromed off the Dumpster and spun into the opposite alley wall, where he doubled over, braced his elbows on his knees, and coughed through a string of bitter curses.

Mandy took two steps toward Radcliff and reached out a hand to help him, then froze again when she saw the spent pepper spray still clutched in her fingers.

His head came up. His watering eyes fixed first on the spray, then traveled up to lock on her. She expected him to bark at her, to snarl bloody murder as he might have done in the hospital.

Instead he exhaled in disgust. "Why am I not surprised?"

He shifted, leaned back against the wall, and reached inside his heavy leather jacket to pull out a cell phone. A single button connected him with whoever he was calling and his watery eyes remained fixed on Mandy as he said, "Stank? We've got a situation. Good news is that I've got some DNA for you. Bad news is, I'm not alone."

THE NEXT HOUR or so was pretty much a blur to Mandy. The cops arrived a few minutes after Radcliff's call, led by Detective James Stankowski, a handsome, dark-haired man whose youthful looks contrasted with his eyes, which were world-weary and cynical.

When Radcliff introduced them, the detective held her hand a moment longer than necessary and asked if she was okay, but before she was able to dredge up a coherent answer, Radcliff hustled her over to a team of paramedics and told her to stay put until he came back for her.

An hour, an ice pack for the bump on her head and a couple of ibuprofen later, she was feeling almost normal—except for the fact that she was surrounded by cops and flashing lights. She'd called Kim on a borrowed cell phone and halfway explained the situation. Only halfway, though, because she wasn't entirely sure yet what exactly had happened. Who was that man? Why had Radcliff been there?

A crowd of curious onlookers had gathered near the mouth of the alley, and they peered in past a string of police tape. A crime scene team had set up powerful lights—the kind the road crews used for night work on the expressway—to illuminate the alley, which looked far smaller and seedier, somehow, than it had in the darkness.

Seated on the edge of an ambulance gurney she didn't really need, Mandy watched the crime scene techs quarter and photograph the area. One stern-faced woman marked the position where the little canister of pepper spray had fallen when she dropped it. The woman picked it up and slipped it into a clear plastic evidence bag, and suddenly the entire scene took on a completely unreal shine.

"I'm dreaming," Mandy said to herself. "I'm really back at work, crashed on one of the couches, dreaming about being in an episode of *CSI: New York*. This isn't real."

"Sorry to disappoint you, but this is as real as it gets," Radcliff's voice said from behind the gurney, startling her.

Mandy turned, then winced and touched her temple when the motion made the world spin. The weakness and the strangeness of it all must've made her more vulnerable than she'd thought, because when she saw him in the light, all she could think was *hel-lo*.

Over the past month, she'd seen him more than she'd wanted to, catching glimpses as he'd gone from meeting to meeting, or when he'd swung by the front desk of the E.R. to leave annoying notes about productivity and cycle time. She'd told herself she shouldn't even notice him, that he was nothing to her now. And, after having only seen him in his starched white coat with The Boss written across the front, she'd almost convinced herself it was the truth.

But now, seeing him up close in his dark-colored tough-guy street clothes with a good dose of five-o'clock shadow, she was suddenly too aware of the strong angle of his jaw and the masculine hardness of his body, too aware of the leashed anger in his eyes.

Too aware that he'd just saved her life.

She had the sudden, undeniable memory of how it had felt to be pressed against him years ago, how they'd come together in heat and need and joy, and how everything else had ceased to exist when they were with each other.

A flush suffused her cheeks when she finally admitted that she'd been lying to herself for the past month. She hadn't been aware of him because he was her boss, or because of their history. She'd noticed him because of *him*. Despite how it had ended, their time together had been amazing, and she'd never found the same sort of connection with another man since, damn it.

The realization sharpened her voice when she turned away from him and snapped, "Don't sneak up on me like that!"

He was silent for a moment, long enough to have her worrying that he'd seen the flare of heat in her eyes. But he made no mention of it, only saying, "Sorry. Didn't mean to scare you." He moved around to stand between her and the crime scene, and then touched her arm, urging her down from the gurney. "Come on. We're leaving."

"It's about time." Resenting the sizzle that sparked at his touch, she yanked away and jumped down off the gurney too quickly, then swayed when the world took a sudden dip to the right.

"Easy there. I've got you." He looped an arm around her waist, and this time when she tried to pull free he merely tightened his hold. "Don't be stupid. It's okay to lean sometimes."

Since when? she thought with a snort at the memory of long-ago conversations that were suddenly too fresh in her mind. But she didn't ask the question aloud, because she'd be damned if she went back there. It was one thing for a few memories to break through in a stressful situation, quite another to acknowledge the memories to the man who starred in them.

So instead, she said, "Where are we going?"

"The Chinatown police station. We'll need to go over your statement." The growl in his voice made Mandy aware of a subtle tension that vibrated through his body.

That, combined with too many other things not lining up, brought latent suspicions flaring to life. A slew of questions suddenly jammed her brain, but she held silent as he led her out of the alley and over to an empty patrol car and ushered her into the backseat, then motioned for her to slide over so he could climb in.

The moment he shut the door, a uniformed officer climbed into the driver's seat, fired up the engine and pulled away from the scene, without a word spoken between the two men. The silent orchestration made Mandy nervous, made her feel as though some unclear fate had already been decided for her.

None of it made any sense. Why had Radcliff been following her? Why the massive police response for a mugging?

And why did the head of the BoGen Emergency Services Department have a police detective on speed-dial?

Making a desperate stab at organizing the questions that spun through her already rattled brain, she said, "Radcliff, what the—"

He held up a hand, cutting her off mid-question. "Not yet, okay? Stankowski will do a better job explaining. He's meeting us at the station."

But though there was a certain logic to that, she got the impression it wasn't the real reason he'd cut her off. When his eyes flicked over to her and away in the glow of passing street-lights, she thought she saw a stir of something in his normally chill expression, making her wonder if he'd felt the faint shimmer of attrac-tion sparking between them back in the alley.

Right. And he's really been pining for you all these years, too, snapped her more rational side. *Grow up.*

Those last two words resonated from the memory of their last night together, making her lean away from him and stare out the window as she fought to reorient herself, knowing that no matter how much she might've wanted to romanticize what had happened between them, he hadn't really wanted her in his life back then any more than he did now. That was fine with her, too, because he was firmly entrenched in the city and its largest hospital. She, on the other hand, was out of there the moment the Meade Fellowship came through.

"We're here," he announced as the officer pulled the patrol car to the curb outside the Chinatown police station. "Come on."

Once the officer opened the rear door, Radcliff climbed out, then held out a hand and waited for her, as though he thought she might collapse, or maybe make a run for it. But she did neither, ignoring his proffered hand to climb out of the car under her own power and stalk up the carved granite steps leading to the police station, leaving him to follow at her heels.

She paused when she reached the main lobby, where a cross-section of Bostonians waited on padded benches, some chatting or reading dog-eared magazines, others glaring off into space.

"Through here." Radcliff led her across the lobby, waving to the two uniformed desk officers, who were attending to a straggling line of people from behind the safety of a chest-high desk and a slab of clear, bullet-proof Plexiglas.

The thought of someone walking into the lobby and shooting up a police station didn't seem nearly as far-fetched to Mandy as it might have only hours earlier, and she suppressed a shiver as she headed down a short hallway in Radcliff's wake.

Nearly to the end of the hall, past a rest room and several offices, Radcliff paused, opened a door and ushered her through into what proved to be a small conference room. The walls were lined with file-stuffed bookshelves, and a large table filled the center of the space, surrounded by a dozen or so utilitarian chairs. An American flag hung in one corner, adding a patriotic dash to the functional space.

There was a second door in the far wall, and before Mandy had gotten her bearings, it swung open and Detective Stankowski strode through.

As before, her first impression was of a darkly handsome man in his early thirties, maybe two or three years older than her. This time, though, she noticed that when his eyes flicked from her to Radcliff and back, the world-weariness in them shifted ever so slightly, giving her the feeling that she was missing something when he took her hand and once again held it a beat too long before guiding her to a chair. As she sat, he said, "Are you sure you're up for this, Dr. Sparks? Parker says you took a pretty good crack to the head back in that alley."

"She's fine," Radcliff broke in. He stepped in front of Stankowski to pull out the chair beside hers, forcing the detective to give way. "Let's get on with this."

Deciding to ignore the brittle undercurrent between the two men for the time being, Mandy waited until Stankowski had taken a seat opposite her, where he arranged a stack of folders and then popped open a slim laptop computer and tapped a few keys. Turning toward Radcliff—she wouldn't think of him as Parker because that was a name he reserved for his friends and she was feeling far from friendly—she narrowed her eyes. "Okay, we're here, so let's have your explanation, and make it good. How about starting with why you followed me tonight?"

Radcliff leaned back in his chair. "You've got it backward—I didn't follow you. I headed for the alley after work for the same reason you did. Lucky for you, we were on the same schedule."

"You—" Mandy broke off, confused. "Why would you care about that alley?"

"For the same reason you do—because that's where Irene Dulbecco was attacked a few days before she died."

"You read my notes?"

He nodded, expression still giving nothing away. "I was in a meeting when she came in, or I would've grabbed her case. As it was, I didn't hear about her until it was too late."

A chill chased its way down Mandy's spine as she began to add it up.

"You've seen something like this before." She glanced at the detective, who was watching her as if expecting—what? What sort of response could she possibly have? "You're working together," she finally said. "But why? Radcliff isn't a cop. At least he wasn't back when—"

"I'm not," he interrupted quickly, making her think he didn't want the detective to know about their past history. He continued, "I dug a bullet out of Stankowski here a few years ago. Ever since then, he's called me when he gets a case that involves something medical." He lifted one shoulder in a half-shrug. "It's a nice change from grant writing. But I work very hard to keep this stuff separate from BoGen."

"Until now," Stankowski said. He spun the laptop around to face Mandy. On the screen was a computer-generated sketch of a figure wearing a dark hooded sweatshirt and a surgical mask. Above the mask, his eyes were light gray and coldly calculating.

Or maybe the calculation was in her mind, borne on the shiver that started in her gut and worked its way through her body, squeezing the air from her lungs until she was almost unable to breathe. "Oh God. That's him. That's the man who attacked me in the alley." She closed her eyes, trying to blot out the fear of memory. "But you already knew that."

When she opened her eyes, the detective had closed the laptop. He nodded.

"How many other people has he attacked?" she whispered through a suddenly dry throat.

"Four including you," Radcliff said, his voice resonating with the deadly sort of calm she'd heard from him only once before, when he'd told her it was over between them. "Of the other three, two are dead and one is missing." He paused a beat. "You know what that makes you?"

Fear spiked, followed by numbing disbelief, but she nodded, glancing from Radcliff to the detective and back. "That makes me your star witness."

"As far as we're concerned, you're a witness," Radcliff said. "As far as the killer is concerned, you're a liability." His voice changed, roughening. "Damn it, why didn't you listen to me? I told you to leave the Dulbecco case alone."

"I couldn't," Mandy whispered. Her breath backed up in her lungs when she remembered the syringe, and that terrible moment when the man had held her down and aimed the needle. If he'd managed to inject her with the clear fluid...

She thought of Irene, who'd writhed in pain despite heavy doses of morphine, and the battery of tests she'd run, only to have all the levels come back within normal limits. Her brain spun with terrible questions, like what in God's name was in that syringe? What would have happened to her if Radcliff hadn't gotten there in time to save her?

More importantly, what was going to happen next?

Chapter Three

"I want you out of here starting now," Parker said. "Take a couple of weeks off. Go someplace nice and chill out." He managed to dredge up what he hoped was a reassuring smile. "I'll clear it with your boss."

But instead of jumping at the chance, as any other member of his staff would have, she shook her head, her face set in familiar stubborn lines. "Not on your life. I'm a doctor and Irene Dulbecco was my patient. If there's any way I can help figure out what was done to her and prevent it from happening to someone else, then that's what I need to do."

And there it is, Parker thought on a bite of temper. He'd once warned her that her damned wide-eyed idealism was going to get her in trouble. He hadn't figured on being there to watch it happen, though, and he hadn't expected the trouble would be of the life-or-death variety.

Maybe he should've known better. Mandy was the sort of person who attracted controversy and chaos—heck, as far as he could tell, she went looking for it. Why else would a prominent surgeon's daughter become the sort of doctor who'd rather prescribe acupuncture than antibiotics? And that was only the latest incarnation of her hidden rebellious streak as far as he was concerned. Back during her rotation through Boston General, she'd driven him crazy by…well, that was just it. She'd driven him crazy at a time when he'd needed to concentrate on himself, and the job.

Now, she was just plain crazy herself. Only a whacko would've gone into that alley alone. If he hadn't been there—

His mind locked on the image of Mandy hospitalized, writhing with a pain he couldn't control, couldn't cure, and the hell of it roughened his tone. "The time off wasn't a suggestion, it was an order. I want you out of here, and I'll see that it happens if I have to load you on a plane to California myself."

"Why California, so I can hide at my daddy's place?" Instead of looking angry or defensive, or any of the half-dozen other emotions he'd been trying to provoke, she rolled her eyes. "You've always been far too impressed with my father and his reputation. Why is that, I wonder?"

Parker gritted his teeth. "What part of *you could be dying right now* do you not understand?"

"I understand it just fine. I'm just not letting it chase me off."

Her words might be defiant, but she paled as she said them, and the pallor brought out the dark smudge of a bruise high on her cheek.

Instead of marring her classic beauty, the injury only enhanced it, reminding Parker that she might be tough enough to stand up to him in the hospital, but she was no physical match for a madman determined to do her harm.

Knowing it, he stood up and leaned over her, bracing his hands on the arms of her chair and crowding her with his body until she leaned back to avoid him. "You're too smart to be this stupid, Mandy. You saw Irene Dulbecco. Do you really want to end up *just like her?*"

In the wake of his shout, angry silence vibrated in the room.

Stankowski finally stepped in. "Okay, that's enough. Parker, sit down and stop being a jerk. And you—" he turned to Mandy "—don't try to be a hero. Parker and I have this under control, and we'll have a better chance of finding this guy if he's not worrying about your safety."

She snorted, but didn't contradict him, instead saying, "I know it's probably no use telling you guys not to worry about me, given the circumstances. But you're not considering the other option."

"There is no other option," Parker said flatly.

"Of course there is," Mandy countered. "In fact I see two." She ticked them off on her fingers. "One, you let me help you. I assume you've tested the bodies for the most common pain-inducing toxins?"

Parker nodded reluctantly. "Yes, we have. That doesn't mean we're looking for an herb, though."

"Aha!" She stabbed a finger at him. "That means you've thought it might be a botanical, or you wouldn't even mention the possibility. Since I know far more than you do about traditional medicine, I can help, and I'm darned well volunteering whether you like it or not. It's my job to heal my patients, and if possible *prevent* them from becoming patients in the first place."

Parker wanted to argue the point but couldn't, because that was pretty much what he'd told himself when he'd first started taking time away from his duties at BoGen in order to help Stankowski. That, and it had appealed to his sense of duty. He'd never wanted to be a cop like his mother had been, but somehow he'd wound up in that world accidentally, and had found he liked it. It had filled a void, offering a challenge he hadn't known he was looking for until it had appeared.

But that was him, not Mandy. She didn't belong in this world any more than he belonged in hers.

"You said there were two options," Stankowski said cautiously. "What's the second?"

"It's simple," she said, though Parker noticed that she'd knotted her fingers tightly together in her lap. "You said it yourself, I'm unfinished business. I've seen the killer's

face, at least some of it, and he has my purse
and keys. You want to catch him, and there's
a pretty good bet he'll come for me sooner
or later. Why not use me—and my apartment—as bait?"

Mandy braced herself for Radcliff to erupt.
Instead the very air around him seemed to
drop a few degrees in temperature. He gritted
his teeth and growled. "Not. An. Option."

Under any other circumstance, with any
other man, she would've snapped at the dic-
tatorial tone. As it was, she found herself
hesitating.

The Radcliff she remembered hadn't possessed such chill control. He'd been loud and
domineering, but she'd quickly learned that
a big chunk of it was a shield, that beneath
the prickles and bluster was a man of fiery
temper and a rare but wonderful humor. At
the time, he'd said that wasn't the real Parker
Radcliff, that she'd brought out something in
him that he couldn't explain. Before things
between them had fallen apart, she'd tried to
help him believe that the other, warmer man
was the real him.

Now, she realized she'd been the one living

in a delusion, or maybe he'd made his belief into a reality, because there was no warmth in the man looking at her now. There was no fire, practically no life in his cold, dark eyes.

A huge shiver crawled up the back of her neck, but she kept her voice even. "I'm not leaving. I think you know I can be as stubborn as you. You can either accept my help, or…" She trailed off, then said simply, "Please let me help. I want to do this. I *need* to do this. I know how it feels not to have answers."

Though there had been plenty of evidence in her mother's death, the LAPD had been unable to make an arrest. Eventually they— and her father—had just let it go.

Mandy, however, still saw her mother's body in her dreams.

Stankowski held up a hand. "Okay, let's take a time-out here." He glanced at his watch and grimaced. "It's nearly midnight and I came on shift early this morning… The crime scene techs will let me know if they get anything from the alley. We're still waiting on some of the tests from Dulbecco's body, but so far the info from her hasn't added anything we didn't already know." He exhaled a frustrated breath. "I'm tired, and I don't think we're going to get anywhere tonight. I vote we call it a night and sleep on things, then reconvene in the morning and make some decisions about Dr. Sparks."

"Call me Mandy, please, and that sounds like a plan to me." Relieved by the prospect of rest, but more determined than ever to be part of the investigation, she said, "I'd like to take a look at the other victims' medical files tonight, if that's okay. Maybe I'll see something that you guys missed." If she could prove her worth, she thought, maybe Stankowski would overrule Radcliff's objections to her involvement.

Why are you so determined to put yourself in the middle of this? her insidious voice of reason asked.

Mandy gritted her teeth and told herself that Irene's husband and kids deserved to know what happened. More importantly, she couldn't just let other people die if there was some way she could help prevent it—she knew how it felt when a family member was murdered. But those answers rang vaguely false because she knew there was a good chance she'd be endangering her own life in the process, making her wonder exactly why she wasn't already halfway to Logan Airport.

She glanced at Radcliff's set profile, and a hard knot gathered in her stomach at the suspicion that she wasn't doing this despite him, but rather *because* of him. Because she felt excited and completely, totally alive for the first time in the four years since she'd left Boston.

"What do you think?" Stankowski asked Radcliff now, seeming immune to his steely-eyed glare. Apparently taking the lack of response as an affirmative, he nodded. "Fine. Mandy can take the charts with her, and we'll meet back here at nine tomorrow to see if she's come up with something we missed."

Mandy exhaled a breath of relief mixed with nerves, and started to rise. Then she hesitated. "Oh, heck. Where am I supposed to stay tonight?" She turned to Stankowski. "Can you have some men watch my apartment?"

"Don't even think of it," Radcliff growled.

"I already have two men on your place," the detective said, ignoring him, "but I don't want you going home, at least not until we have a real plan." He glanced at Radcliff, and a glint entered his tired eyes when he said, "I've got a spare room. You're welcome to bunk with me for tonight."

"No." Radcliff stood. "She's coming home with me. End of discussion."

OF COURSE it wasn't the end of the discussion, because Mandy had to protest that she didn't need a babysitter, while Stank kept offering his spare room. Parker figured the detective's insistence was partly designed to annoy him, and partly because, as he'd suspected, Mandy's California blond good looks were right up Stank's alley.

Not liking the gleam in the detective's eyes any more than he liked the idea of Mandy spending the night in her own place, Parker finally snapped, "Either we do it my way or we spend the next hour arguing. Personally I'd rather grab some dinner and hit the sack."

That pretty much ended the conversation, which should have been a relief. The only problem was that once he'd won the argument, Parker was left with a prize he didn't want.

Or rather, one he shouldn't want, but did.

He tried to work it out in his head as they caught a cab and rode to his place in a tense silence broken only by the strains of Mozart coming from the driver's radio.

It made logical sense for Mandy to come home with him. He had a spare bedroom that was far nicer than the closet-size guest room in Stank's place, and he'd be nearby if she had any questions on the medical charts or the tests that'd been run on the victims so far.

He didn't want her involved in the case, but he had to admit that her knowledge of herbal medicine was far greater than his, and he was certain they weren't dealing with a garden-variety toxin of the sort typically used for murder, such as warfarin, cyanide or arsenic.

Besides, even if Mandy was safely stashed at Stank's place, he'd still be worried about her…and that was the problem.

He didn't want to worry about her, didn't want to care one way or the other about her, but blind rage had hit him the moment he'd realized what was going down in that alley. Hell, he'd felt the jolt earlier in the day, when he'd gone toe-to-toe with her in the hallway at work. Then again, he'd never been able to control his responses around Mandy. They weren't good for each other, but they'd been damn good together. Now, with the prospect of spending the night in close quarters, he knew one thing if he knew anything: he was going to have to keep his hands to himself.

With that vow firmly in mind as the taxi driver pulled up to the curb in front of his Beacon Hill town house, he got out and paid the driver.

"Come on." He scanned their night-quiet surroundings as he gestured for Mandy to precede him up the brick walkway, but there was nothing suspicious about the well-lit area or the passing cars. Still, he didn't relax until he got the front door unlocked and checked the security system, which was green across the board.

He reset the system and locked the door, expecting to feel a sense of relief that they were home safe. Instead his disquiet only increased as he turned toward Mandy, who stood just inside the door, swaying on her feet as though she was about ready to drop from exhaustion and the stress of the day.

She caught his eye and deliberately looked away, scanning his town house.

He'd had the whole place done over when he bought it a few months after his divorce was finalized, and the result was three levels of late eighteenth century period-correct hardwood floors, exposed beams and horse-hair plaster, offset with modern touches of marble, chrome and glass. The decorator he'd hired had gone with greens and blues, and from the entryway the splashes of color were visible both on the second floor, which was level with the front door, and the upper level, which had been partly cut away to form a balcony of sorts surrounding the cathedral ceiling of the sitting room on the second floor.

He'd left the bottom floor untouched and used it as his gym, but the main floors practically screamed "understated opulence," which was what he'd been going for.

Now, though, he wondered what Mandy saw when she looked around. And, realizing that her response mattered far more than it should, he realized something else.

She was the first woman, other than the

decorator and the cleaning lady, that he'd invited into his home.

"Nice." Mandy hummed a note under her breath. "Very nice." But there was something guarded in her voice when she said, "Did you bring the files on the other victims?"

He nodded. "Yeah. You can have a look at them, let me know if you see anything we missed."

But he didn't hand them over, didn't move except to draw in a deep breath, one that brought her scent to him, a mix of shampoo and woman he'd told himself he'd forgotten long ago. Now, though, it was inescapable, and it triggered memories he could've sworn were gone forever, memories of heat and chaos, and a blond-haired girl who'd—both then and now—stirred him up more than had been comfortable, or wise.

"I don't think this is going to work," he said. "You and me working together on this…it's just not a good idea."

Her eyes narrowed. "Why not?"

"Because of this." Before she knew what he intended, hell before *he* was conscious of

making the move, Parker crossed the distance
separating them.

And kissed her.

Chapter Four

Mandy froze in shock the moment Radcliff's lips touched hers.

The first thought that flitted through her mind was a panicked sort of relief that the attraction she'd been feeling with increasing sharpness throughout the day wasn't one-sided.

Her second thought never materialized; it was lost beneath a wash of heat when his mouth slanted across hers.

She parted her lips and kissed him back, her body responding before her mind had a chance to catch up. Warning buzzers sounded dimly in the back of her brain, but she couldn't bring herself to care just then. She was awash in sensation, suddenly drowning beneath a wave of need.

The stubble of his faint beard rasped

beneath her fingertips when she lifted a hand to touch his jaw, urging him closer. She closed her eyes and tried not to go boneless when his tongue touched hers and every neuron she possessed flared to life simultaneously on a shouted thought: *Finally!*

Finally he held her close, his touch arrogant and possessive, like the man himself. Finally his body pressed against hers and his scent filled her nostrils—a poignantly familiar blend of hospital soap and the spiciness that was his alone.

She melted against him, curled herself around him and hung on for a kiss that began at the point where their mouths fused, but then spiraled outward, becoming far more than itself.

What started as taste and touch quickly became heat and need. Desire had her sliding her hands down his neck to his upper arms, where she dug her fingers into the heavy leather of his jacket until she felt the tight muscles beneath. Lust coiled, hard and demanding, warning her that she'd been lying to herself for the past month, and maybe for the four years before that.

She'd told herself she'd gotten over him, but she'd been wrong. Otherwise, it would've taken more than a kiss before she was right back in the same place she'd been before, half-blind with desire, and ready to give up anything to be with him.

This time when the warning buzzers shrilled, she heard them loud and clear.

She froze in his arms, then pulled her lips from his. They were twined together in an intimate embrace, with her back against the entryway wall, one of his thighs wedged between hers, and her fingers digging into his arms as though he was the only thing keeping her on her feet. "Wait," she said, her voice coming out thin and breathy.

In the hallway light he'd flicked on when they'd come in, she could see his pulse pounding at the side of his neck. A dark, indefinable emotion gleamed in his eyes momentarily, one that looked very much like anger and had nerves fisting in her stomach. Then his expression blanked and he stepped away from her, leaving her to lean against the wall for support.

"Like I said, this is a bad idea." His voice

was thick, rasping with desire. "I can't work with you."

His words cut deep, but still the memories crowded her, brought by the taste and feel of him, and by the lure of the illicit, the sense that they shouldn't be doing what they were doing. Unfortunately she was enough of a grown-up now to admit that the forbidden aspects had always been part of the lure.

You're better than that, she told herself, and meant it. *You're stronger and smarter than you were before. Believe it.*

Because she believed it, she lifted her chin and met his dark-eyed stare. "Why won't it work, because we're attracted to each other? Please. That didn't stop you from kicking me to the curb four years ago. I'd like to think I can return the favor now by not letting it get personal if we're forced to work in close quarters for the next few days."

"I hardly call what we just did 'not getting personal,'" Radcliff said without an ounce of humor. "Personally I call it a hell of a distraction, and I'm not in a position to be distracted right now."

Mandy was far from feeling casual, but

managed to interject a hint of boredom into her tone. "So control yourself. You kissed me, not the other way around. It's not like I took two steps inside your door and started stripping."

She had once before, though, in a different time and place. They'd slept together one time, and he'd tried to end it, saying he wasn't in a good place, that she deserved better. Thinking him overly noble, she'd invited herself over and seduced him. The memory of it crept into her brain, bringing a warm flush to the skin of her face and arms.

From the glint in his eyes, she wasn't the only one taking a little trip down memory lane. That guess was confirmed when he said, "No, but you weren't exactly complaining just now."

"I can enjoy locking lips without letting it mess with my head these days." She raised an eyebrow. "I should probably thank you for that."

"Don't." He turned away from her suddenly, and yanked off his jacket in a surge of motion that was at odds with his usual rigid control. He looped the jacket onto a rack of hooks near the door and held out a hand for her parka. "Let's go sit down. I think we need to talk this through."

She handed over the coat, but stood her ground. "Let's not. We kissed and we enjoyed it—that's no surprise. Sex was never the problem between us, was it?" She shook her head, answering her own question. "No, our problems were partly the gap in our ages and experiences, and partly a difference in expectations, so let's deal with both of those things right up-front. One—" she ticked off the point on a finger "—there's no more experience gap. I've learned what I needed to know—and then some—over the past four years. And because of that experience, I don't expect anything from you except a fair shake when it comes time for you to write my recommendation letter."

He hung up her parka, movements deliberate, as though he was buying himself a moment. When he turned back to her, she read nothing more than faint impatience on his face, making her wonder if she'd imagined the darker, stronger emotions there before, whether she'd once again been projecting her own feelings onto him.

Not again, she told herself. Four years earlier she'd vowed to never again get herself caught in that sort of trap. Since then, she'd spelled out the terms of each relationship ahead of time, so there would be no surprises, no disappointments.

The system had worked before. It would work this time, as well.

"I know you don't want me involved with you and Detective Stankowski on this case," she said. "And I can't say I blame you…but I'm also not willing to step aside. You said it yourself—this guy has my ID and my keys, and the likelihood is that he's not just going to walk away and forget about me. That makes it my best interest to help you catch him."

This time, she let the silence draw out between them.

Radcliff broke first, shaking his head and turning away. "We both know that's circular logic, but I'm not going to waste energy trying to talk you out of it. Come on into the kitchen. I'll fix us something while you go over the files. That way I'm in shouting distance if you have any questions."

Without another word, he grabbed his soft-sided briefcase off the table where he'd dumped it when they'd first come in, and strode into the main living space of the town house.

Mandy stood in the entryway, rattled by his change in tactics. And that, she realized quickly, had been the point. He wanted her off balance and guessing, because if she wasn't in control of the conversation, then that meant he was, and if there was one thing that hadn't changed about Radcliff over the years, it was that he liked to be in control of the things—and the people—around him.

Muttering under her breath, she followed him to the kitchen.

The town house was a narrow structure that was three levels tall and only one room wide, with the rooms on each floor arranged in a line, shotgun-style. She passed through the first room of the middle floor, where tall ceilings, cream-colored walls and polished wooden beams gave the impression of lightness even though it was dark outside and few lamps were lit. To her left, one staircase descended below street level and another climbed to a third story, the spaces overlapping so the treads of the upper staircase soared above the lower stairs, all in warm, burnished wood that spoke of age and permanence. The load-bearing walls had been turned into arches and pillars, so two of the three rooms that had originally made up the main floor had become one large sitting area.

There, reproduction couches and chairs gave the look of antiques with modern lounge-about comfort, and were nearly buried beneath cushions and boldly colored blankets. A fireplace flanked one side of the room, a wide plasma TV hung on the opposite wall. Startling color and vibrance came from a profusion of green plants that hung in pots, sat on shelves and grew from wide clay buckets on the floor, all looking green and healthy, some even with blossoms—delicate pink and fire-engine red—though it was January.

Mandy automatically cataloged the plants, noting that many were varieties that needed daily care.

The thought of Parker Radcliff puttering around checking soil pH and moisture was so jarring she immediately knew he had to have a plant service, and probably rode them as hard as he did his staff. There was no way he took care of the greenery himself. Frankly she was surprised he'd bothered to install them in the first place. *No doubt the plants were the decorator's doing,* Mandy thought, feeling a hint of amusement at the contrast between his place and her inexpensive apartment.

Most of her possessions were still in boxes, and her decorating efforts had been limited to hanging a few framed art posters. His place, on the other hand, was practically a showpiece.

When she reached the kitchen, she saw that the hardwood floors gave way to blue-green tilework, which added a splash of color to the cream paint and warm wood cabinets. The expensive fittings and appliances were brushed steel and the counters black marble, but additional touches of blue and green made the room feel warm rather than cold.

The man inside the kitchen, though, looked anything but warm. Frustration had deepened the hard lines beside his mouth and tightened the skin between his brows, making his expression thunderous and forbidding.

Any sane woman with an ounce of self-preservation in her soul would've backed away.

Mandy stepped forward, crossing the wide kitchen until she stood just opposite him near the sink. She lifted her chin and forced her eyes to match him chill for chill. "You left before I was finished with the ground rules."

"I know." He turned and crossed to a granite-topped island, and busied himself with the cold cuts he'd laid out, assembling sandwiches with precisely controlled motions. "We don't need rules here because there's nothing to legislate. I'm keeping an eye on you for the next day or so, that's all. If you can give us something new from those—" he nodded to the medical files he'd laid out on a small table in the corner "—all the better. If not, we'll figure out something longer term for your protection."

Irritation flared, even though she knew his rundown wasn't all that far off the reality of the situation. "That's not what I'm talking about and you know it. Or have you conveniently forgotten laying one on me a few minutes ago?"

He glanced at her, his eyes darkening with a flash of heat that was there and gone so quickly she might've missed it if she hadn't been feeling it herself.

"It'll be a long time before I forget kissing you again," he said. "But that just proves my point. There's no way we can work closely together without remembering what we had together, and being tempted to go there all over again."

Mandy gritted her teeth. "I'm not a green intern anymore, *Dr.* Radcliff. I'm an experienced E.R. physician who can hold her own, regardless of the situation."

"We're not exactly in a typical E.R. scenario right now, are we?" Emphasizing the point, he slid one of the sandwiches he'd made onto a plate, and handed it to her, then jerked his chin toward a pair of stools set into the intimate corner breakfast nook. "Have a seat."

Their knees bumped as they settled into the niche, sitting too close together. Mandy was just about to suggest they move out into the main room when he caught her eye and lifted one eyebrow in challenge, as if to say, *you think this won't be an issue? Prove it.*

So she settled into the breakfast nook and told herself not to notice how nice it felt to have her legs pressed up against his beneath the table, or how much warmer and safer she felt now than she had an hour ago, back at the police station.

That comfort was an illusion, she knew. He could—and would—yank it away at any second.

Don't get used to being around him, she reminded herself. He might not be willing to let her set the ground rules for their association, but she'd damn well set some for herself. Rule one: she wasn't letting Radcliff call all the shots this time. Rule two: she wasn't letting herself be marginalized if she really, truly thought she could help solve her patient's murder and prevent others—including herself—from being harmed. And the third and most important rule: she wasn't getting emotionally involved with him all over again. She'd already been there, done that, bought the heartache.

The chemistry between them might still pack a punch, but that didn't mean she had to stand there and take it. She was older now, and wiser. And, she thought with an inner grimace, if she told herself that a few thousand more times, she might actually believe it, despite all kissing evidence to the contrary.

Sighing, she pushed her plate aside to make room for the medical files she'd carried with her. "Okay, so where do we start?"

PARKER VETOED his first three responses to a question that seemed innocuous enough on the surface, but in reality had far too many layers. Then again, he thought, she might've meant it exactly as it sounded, and he was the one adding layers and complications that didn't need to be there.

He was the one who'd initiated the kiss. He was the one complicating things.

For a guy who'd ended their potentially messy relationship before it'd gotten too serious four years earlier, he wasn't doing a very good job of keeping it simple this time around. Because knowing it made him edgy and irritable, he scowled and did what he did best—focused on the things he could control. Like medicine. And information.

He frowned down at the hospital files. "My initial thought was that if we could identify the weapon, it could lead us to the killer."

"I take it you changed your mind?"

"No. Just haven't had much luck figuring

out which toxin he's using. I've ruled out most of the usual poisons and environmental toxins we'd associate with intense pain. I even tried a few really out there theories, but so far everything's come back within normal limits." And if that both ticked him off and fascinated him, he figured the first emotion was his medical training speaking, and the second was his mother's heritage. She'd been a good cop, and had nearly been among the first women to make detective in the Pittsburgh force.

He figured curiosity would be a legacy she'd enjoy, just as she would approve of his detachment, because it had been her emotional involvement in a case that had gotten her killed.

Mandy tapped the files. "Did you find any connections among the vics?"

"Vics?" he repeated, then scowled. "You've been watching too many cop shows again." The reminder of that frivolous vice only served to underscore the gap in their ages, as it had done before. She watched junk TV, while he read six scientific journals cover to cover per week, trying to keep himself abreast of the latest breakthroughs.

"Oh, for the love of…Give me that." She reached out, flipped open the topmost file and read aloud. "Julian George, retired widower, sixty-six years old. History of heart attack and high blood pressure, neither of which explain why he ended up at Mass Medical with sudden onset, acute systemic pain." She paused and glanced at him. "In other words, he hit the Mass Med E.R. because everything hurt for no reason. Same reason Irene's husband brought her to BoGen."

Parker nodded and picked up the story from memory. "Julian was in the city for the weekend, visiting his daughter and her children. When he and the daughter started getting on each other's nerves she sent him to pick up dinner on the edge of Chinatown. He was on his way back when he was mugged two blocks over from your alley."

"It's hardly *my* alley," she retorted, but bit into her sandwich rather than saying anything else.

"Before that," Parker said, flipping to a file that held a police report rather than medical charts. "Twenty-six-year-old Missy Prieta was mugged one street over on her way home from a lo-mein run. She filed a police report ten days ago. Two days after that, her roommates filed a missing persons report, and so far we've got nothing."

Mandy winced. "Poor Missy." Neither of them bothered with the optimistic platitudes. Odds were that Missy Prieta's body would come to light sooner or later.

"She was just about your age." Parker glanced from the photo to Mandy and back again. "Similar coloring, too."

"Don't try to make me part of a pattern just because it suits your needs," she said with unexpected steel. "The only reason he went after me is that I stuck my nose where it didn't belong…or rather, where he didn't want it. And quite frankly, the same could be said of your nose, too."

"True," he agreed, "but one of us is licensed to carry concealed, and it's not you."

That earned him a long, speculative look. "You're packing heat?"

Parker snorted at the TV-ism. "Not at the moment, no." But he would be for the foreseeable future, because he'd be damned if he stood by again with nothing but his fists as weapons when the killer took another crack at her.

And if the thought of that brought more anger and determination than it should have, given that they were nothing to each other, he was the only one who needed to know it.

Oblivious to his thoughts, Mandy pressed, "So what are you thinking about these deaths? Infection or poison?"

"It's almost certainly a toxin." Parker retrieved Julian George's file from her and flipped through the notes again, though he'd practically memorized them already. "Even though the killer wears a mask and gloves, he isn't bothering with eye protection. I'm guessing the get-up is for the scare factor, or to give his victims something to focus on other than his face."

"I'm sorry to say that it worked." Mandy grimaced. "I can picture a guy in powder-free gloves and a mask, with a 10 cc syringe and a 10-bore needle. That pretty much had my attention."

"The other reason to think toxin rather than pathogen is that to the best of our knowledge, nobody who came into contact with the victims has gotten sick." Parker was vaguely surprised to realize it was helping him to work through the argument once more, in front of a critical audience he knew would call him on the disconnects.

Rather than admit it, he bit into his dinner, chewing and swallowing mechanically without tasting the sandwich.

"There are a few bioengineered bugs that are one-shot deals, designed to infect the initial host but not spread beyond that person," Mandy said slowly, staring at Julian George's file with a faint wrinkle at her brow, as though she feared she was missing something important.

"True," Parker agreed, "but it'd be tough for a street crook to get his hands on an engineered virus of that caliber."

"Not if he's working for someone who can supply the bug." Mandy paused, and the frown lines smoothed out as she shrugged. "You're right, though. A toxin is far more likely. Question is, which one?"

"That's the rub." Parker slid a blue folder from beneath the others and laid it on top of the pile, then gathered the plates and loaded them into the dishwasher, saying over his shoulder, "That folder has the results from all the tests I've run on the samples from Julian George, and partial results from today's tests on Irene Dulbecco's remains. Have a look and tell me what else we need to do in order to catch the latest fad in toxic herbal cure-alls."

Her eyes flashed at the dig, but she said simply, "There are more things on heaven and earth, Radcliff…"

Figuring he'd let her have the last line—for now—he headed upstairs. Not because he was retreating, per se, but because he knew that if they shared space any longer, he might do something very, very stupid.

Like start thinking they could pick up where they'd left off four years earlier.

Chapter Five

Mandy went over the files until her lower back ached, her eyes went blurry and her head started to pound, but she didn't give in to the discomfort, because she knew the answer had to be there somewhere.

All of the test levels had come back within normal limits, true, but some were skewed to the high or low ends of the "normal" spectrum. There was a pattern in the small test irregularities. She was sure of it. She just wasn't sure what that pattern was telling her yet.

When she reached the end of Julian George's file, she flipped back to the beginning and started over. As she did so, she yawned, popping her ears and spiking the headache into a quick bolt of pain behind her right eye.

"Ow." Wincing, she rubbed her eyes, then

glanced around the kitchen, wondering where Radcliff kept his aspirin.

She jolted when she found him standing in the doorway, leaning against the wall with his arms crossed over his chest. He'd changed into a gray Harvard sweatshirt and a soft-looking pair of jeans that were worn at the knees and frayed at the cuffs. On any other man she would've figured they were his handyman jeans. On Radcliff, she had to assume they'd been artistically aged for some designer label, because she could hardly see him with his head under the sink, cursing at the plumbing.

And if for a moment she could picture exactly that, and the image brought a tug of longing for the domesticity it implied, then that was nothing more than a product of the late night and the strange situation she'd found herself caught up in.

"What?" he said, raising an eyebrow.

Realizing she was smiling for no good reason, she waved off his question. "Nothing," she said at first, then was forced to laugh at herself. "I was just thinking that when I got up this morning, if anyone had told me I'd be spending the night at your place, I would've called them a liar…after I got done falling off my chair, doubled over with hysterical laughter."

He frowned. "I'd hardly call this a laughing matter."

Refusing to be bullied for even an instant—because she knew if she gave in this time she'd be playing catch up from then on—she lifted her chin and met him stare for stare. "Of course you wouldn't. I, however, don't see humor as a sign of immaturity or an indication that the other person doesn't understand the severity of the situation. I see it as a coping mechanism. You should try it sometime."

"I cope just fine." He pushed away from the door frame and crossed the kitchen in three long strides, until he was near enough that she could feel the heat coming off his body, and sense his irritation with her, with the situation.

"If you're trying to intimidate me, it's not working." She looked back down at the notes, dismissing him with a wave. "You're my boss at work, not here, so you can't order me around. If you're not going to help, then go away."

"Trust me, I'm helping." Without a by-your-leave, he swept up the files, snapped them shut and tucked them under his arm.

"Hey!" she yelped, anger spiking quickly. "What's the deal?"

"The deal is that it's nearly two in the morning and the only thing keeping you going is adrenaline and sheer bloody-mindedness." He paused, and made a visible effort to soften his delivery when he said, "Shut it off for a few hours, okay? Unless we get seriously lucky, it'll all still be here in the morning."

Mandy shot up from her chair intending to rip into him, but had to pause and grab onto the edge of the counter when the world took a couple of spins around her. That got her heart rate up, which made her head hammer and her vision blur.

She hung on to the counter for a second, breathing through her nose. When everything settled down again, she exhaled. "Okay, maybe you've got a point."

Realistically she'd been on her feet since early that morning. Sure, she used to go thirty or forty hours at a stretch during her training years, but she'd gotten out of the habit since then. Besides, the fear and adrenaline from the attack had probably taken more out of her than she'd acknowledged, even to herself.

Radcliff nodded, thankfully not pushing it. "The guest room is upstairs, first door on the right. The bathroom is across the hall, but the shower in there is pretty anemic, so you're probably better off using the one in the master bath, straight through at the end of the hall."

"Where will you be?" she asked, not caring what he read into the question.

"For the immediate future? Downstairs in the weight room, keeping middle age at bay." He paused, as though wanting her to look at him and see—what? An older man? A fit man? He was both of those things, as well she knew. Problem was, her body didn't seem to care about a few years age difference, and muscles were muscles, and he had plenty of them. When she didn't say anything, he cocked a brow. "I won't walk in on you while you're showering, if that's what you're worried about."

"I'm not worried, I'm trying to figure out the ground rules," she snapped suddenly beyond tired, beyond frustrated. "I might've had a seriously long day, but that doesn't change the fact that I'm getting mixed signals here. For the past month we've done a pretty good job of ignoring each other and getting along at work, and then this morning, you march up to me and—oh." She broke off as their early-morning encounter rearranged itself in her head, taking on new meaning. "You'd just found out about Irene, hadn't you?"

He nodded. "I knew the moment I heard who'd signed her in that there was going to be trouble. You don't let things go easily."

"You've got that right." Mandy paused, squelching the faint sting of disappointment. "So I'll accept that this morning's little encounter was damage control, not a come-on. But the way you refused to let me go home with Stankowski and kissed me when we got here, then said it was a mistake but refused to discuss the situation…" She shook her head. "Forgive me if I'm looking for a few definitions of terms here, but this is all making my head spin."

"The concussion is making your head spin." But he backed off, returning to his former position leaning against the door frame with his arms folded across his chest, right over the Harvard logo. "And you're the one who used to be all about spontaneity and letting the chips fall where they may. Since when do you want rules?"

"Since I got burned by assumptions," she said quietly, deciding to let him interpret that however he wanted, because at least some of his answers would be right. "So if you'll indulge me, I think we can agree on the following." She ticked the points off on her fingers. "One, because of—or perhaps despite—our past history, there's some residual chemistry between us. Two, neither one of us is looking for a relationship right now. You don't want to make your life any more complicated than it already is—which I can respect—and I need to focus on the fellowship. It's still a year away, but I'm not letting anything distract me or make me think twice when it comes time to leave."

When she paused, he nodded. "No arguments here, but you've left out an option."

"I'm getting to it." She added a third finger. "Three, you may be an expert at keeping things simple and forgetting your patients—

and your women—the moment they're out the door, but that's not how I work."

He nodded, expression guarded. "That's… blunt."

She lifted one shoulder even as a tremor of nerves took root in her stomach. "I don't mean to be rude." Maybe she did, a little. She hadn't liked hearing the front-desk rumors about Radcliff and the rotating cast of younger women he dated, which had only further cheapened what'd happened between them. "The point is that I'm a long-term kind of girl. I keep my friends as long as possible and I keep in touch with all my family members, even the ones I wouldn't necessarily like if I met them at a party."

The irritation on his face gave way to sardonic amusement. "If you give this speech every time a guy asks you out, I can't imagine you date much."

"There's no speech," she said stiffly, unwilling to admit that he'd struck a nerve. "I don't go out with men with whom there's no possible future, because when I fall, I fall hard and it hurts too much to have the trampoline yanked out from underneath me before I land."

A faint shadow flitted across his expression, but he said, "Are there any more rules I should know about?"

"Not about this, no."

"Then I'll say good night. Sleep well and I'll see you in a few hours. Our shift starts at nine, and we're meeting with Stankowski at seven."

Like he needed to remind her of that, Mandy thought, unreasonably irritated when he turned and exited the kitchen, leaving her feeling as though he couldn't have cared less about her rules or the reasons behind them.

Then again, why should he? He'd already said they shouldn't work together, that there was chemistry between them but no future. She'd only been telling him what he already knew.

She was tired, that was all, Mandy thought, pressing her aching forehead to the cool granite countertop and closing her eyes for a second. Her defenses were low. That was the only reason she wanted to burst into tears, the only reason she was tempted to chase after him and poke at him until… what? What response did she want from him?

She couldn't articulate it, but she knew damn well she hadn't gotten it just now.

"No big surprise there," she whispered to herself. "Parker Radcliff never could give you what you wanted."

Or rather, he'd given her the raunchy, no-holds-barred sex they'd both wanted, but he hadn't been able to give her the closeness she needed. Unfortunately the guys she'd met since then who'd been willing to give her the closeness she'd wanted hadn't even registered on the raunchy sex Richter scale, leaving her just as lonely and dissatisfied as she'd been without them, making her think she would've been better off having never met Radcliff, having never tangled with him, fought with him, made love with him…

"Argh!" she finally growled in frustration, when old and new memories crowded too close and fused together in her head, creating a hot, wanting mess that left her jumbled up and far too needy for her own good.

Knowing her best bet was to sleep it off, she headed upstairs, scrounged aspirin out of the medicine cabinet and used the anemic guest shower rather than braving the master suite. She set the alarm clock on the bedside table for 6:00 a.m. so she'd be wide-awake by the time she had to face him again. It wasn't until she stripped off her sweater and jeans and a small object fell to the carpet that memory flashed and she realized she'd made a potentially big mistake.

"Oh, crap." She picked the minidisk up off the floor and stared at it, seeing once again the initials ID, and now a new scratch added to the one on the back, no doubt from the disk having spent half a day in her back pocket.

She'd forgotten all about it. She should've given it to Stankowski hours ago. Now it was in even worse shape than it had been before, maybe even unreadable.

Staring at the disk, Mandy considered her options. She could go downstairs and interrupt Parker's workout, but she wasn't sure what sort of device they'd need to read the minidisk—if it was even readable—and couldn't imagine he'd wake Stankowski at this hour of the night. And maybe it was cowardly, but she didn't really want to face either of them again until morning, so she set the minidisk on the night table next to the clock and lay down, expecting her racing mind to keep her awake.

She was asleep within minutes.

THE NEXT MORNING, Parker was on his third cup of coffee before Mandy put in an appearance, but it wasn't the burn of acid or caffeine that had him scowling as she came down the stairs. It wasn't even the exhaustion that pulled at him, courtesy of a restless night spent thinking of her, and what would've happened to her if he'd been a few minutes later to reach the alley the day before.

No, what disturbed him was the way his heart bumped in his chest when he saw her, the way his eyes locked on to her and wouldn't let go and the way it clicked inside him, a sense of *there you are*, as if he'd been looking for her a long time now and hadn't even realized it.

He didn't like the feelings, didn't trust them. He liked who he was, liked his life just fine.

At least he had until he'd seen Mandy's name in the pile of résumés submitted for an opening in his department. Since then he'd been looking at his life differently, and he didn't like that. He didn't like change, didn't like being unsettled, but that was exactly what he was feeling as she hit the bottom step, turned the corner and paused when she found him standing in the kitchen archway, staring at her.

Or maybe "glaring" was a better description, he acknowledged inwardly. Instead of being warned by his expression and treading carefully, as anyone else in his life would have with the possible exception of Stankowski, she scowled right back at him.

"I can see five hours of bunktime did nothing to improve your mood," she said. "Can we wait on the fight until I've had coffee, or do you want to just throw down here in the living room?"

The lurid images that sprang to mind at her offer had nothing to do with fighting, which only deepened his scowl.

Seeing that she was holding an envelope, he gestured. "What's that?"

She flushed. "I have a confession. I picked this up off the ground in the alley right before the attack. I must've shoved it in my pocket, I don't really remember. Honestly, I didn't remember about the disk at all until I found it last night while I was getting undressed." She passed him the envelope. "It's a disk of some sort, labeled 'ID.' That might not mean anything, but then again maybe it means something. I was thinking it might've fallen out of Irene's bag during the struggle."

"That's just great. I can only imagine what the fabric of your pocket did to any prints." He looked inside the envelope and saw two big scratches marring the disk. "I think it's trashed, but we should run this over to Stankowski first thing." He held out his own mug of coffee, knowing they liked it exactly the same. "You can drink it in the cab. I figured you'd want to stop at your place on the way in, get a change of clothes, that sort of thing, so I called Stank. He said his team didn't see any suspicious activity on their drive-bys, and we're clear to go in."

The detective had also told Parker to wear his gun and keep Mandy in sight at all times, but he didn't figure she needed to know that before she'd had her morning caffeine hit.

Gratitude flashed in her eyes and she nodded. "Thanks." She took the coffee, her fingers brushing lightly against his. "Thanks for this, too."

He merely jerked his chin at the door. "Grab your coat and let's go."

When they got in the cab he flagged down, she gave an address several blocks south of Boston General. Then she borrowed his cell phone and called the manager of her apartment building, who agreed to meet them and give her the spare key to her place.

Parker frowned when they neared their destination. "Pretty sketchy neighborhood."

The tall brick apartment buildings that lined either side of the road were indistinguishable from one another, pushed up close to the cracked sidewalks. Garbage cans sat willy-nilly, some having rolled into the road, and a scattering of paper and empties gave the area an abandoned, unloved feeling. Parked cars were jammed hood-to-trunk, and represented an odd mix of junkers, muscle cars and late model pickups and SUVs. The latter had Parker's cynical side thinking the illegals market was alive and well in Mandy's neighborhood.

"Don't be a snob," she said tartly. "We

can't all live in mansions in Beverly Hills or million-dollar town houses on Beacon Street. In fact, some of us wouldn't want to." When he opened his mouth to respond, she steamrollered right over him, saying, "It's not fancy, but the neighbors look out for each other. It's as safe as anything else I could afford. I need to save as much as I can so I'll have enough to see me through two years in China. The fellowship pays travel and housing, but the luxuries—like food—will be up to me."

"You could've gotten a nicer place and shared it with a roommate," he said as they climbed out of the cab and he paid the driver.

"Please. I'm twenty-nine years old. I think I've outgrown the roommate thing." She headed for the front door of her building, calling over her shoulder, "Besides, I didn't figure I'd be here much. Rumor has it that my boss is a slave driver."

"Somebody should talk to him about that." He grinned because she seemed to need the humor. What had she called it? A coping mechanism.

Well, she seemed to be coping, but he had

to wonder for how long. She was tough and stubborn, but the murders had to be hitting close to home after what had happened to her mother. She'd never told him the entire story, but from what he'd gathered, the experience had pretty much destroyed her relationship with her father, who had remarried quickly and gotten on with his life while teenage Mandy had still needed to grieve, and was still searching for the closure that had never come.

Parker could only hope that need wouldn't drive her to do something foolish—and dangerous—now.

THE TRIP to Mandy's apartment was uneventful, and the stopover at the police station wasn't much different. Stankowski hadn't blasted her for forgetting about the disk; in fact, he hadn't seemed all that interested in it, simply passing it off to a tech with instructions to see what he could get off the thing.

Then he'd turned back to the medical files, and Mandy was forced to admit she hadn't had a lightbulb moment on what toxin had killed the victims. Although she planned on making some calls and maybe ordering an additional test or two, she really hadn't been able to add anything to what Parker had already told the detective.

Because of that, she expected that Detective Stankowski would thank her for her interest and tell her to get lost. She'd been surprised when he'd told her to keep digging, but Parker's reaction hadn't been at all unexpected. He'd snapped and snarled, and all but ordered her to keep her nose out of police business. When she'd pointed out he wasn't a cop, either, he'd lapsed into cool silence, broken only when they reached Boston General and he loaded her down with a dozen charts and told her to get the hell to work.

She did exactly that, because she was a healer first and foremost, but that didn't stop her from making a couple of calls in between cases. As far as she was concerned, there were a few strings the men hadn't thought to pull because, well, they were men. She wasn't hampered by that problem.

It wasn't until three hours later, when she was finishing up the stitches on six-year-old Tommy McGregor, who had tied a bed sheet around his neck as a cape and tried to "fly" off the family's raised front porch, that the intercom pinged and one of the front desk staffers told her she had a call.

Mandy took a few minutes to go over Tommy's aftercare instructions with his frazzled mother and sent them off with a lollipop each before she grabbed the wall phone.

"Hello, Mrs. Stone? This is Dr. Sparks over at Boston General. Thank you so much for returning my call. I got your name and number from Steve Dulbecco, and I was wondering if we could meet?"

Five minutes later, Mandy headed out the door. She stopped by the front desk, where a faintly ditzy and hugely pregnant staffer named Aimee was manning the phones. "I'm going to grab a cup of coffee in the Atrium. Be back in ten minutes. I'm on the beeper if anyone needs me, but the load's pretty light. You should be fine."

She was out the door before the startled woman could respond. Mandy knew she should call over to Parker's office and ask him to come along on the interview, but she didn't because she didn't want to argue over the calls she'd made, and she wasn't sure she wanted to spend any more time than necessary with him.

Besides, Irene's best friend might be more open to talking about intimate details with another woman than with a man.

Chapter Six

Down in the Atrium, Mandy saw a middle-aged woman in a puffy red parka waiting near the café entrance where they'd arranged to meet. Crossing to meet her, Mandy extended her hand. "Mrs. Stone?"

The woman nodded. "Call me Millie, please."

Her handshake was tentative, her knuckles large and gnarled, suggesting advanced arthritis, though she was only in her forties. She was as short and round as Irene had been tall and lean. Her hair was curly brown and her face was open and probably cheerful under normal circumstances. As she and Mandy ordered their coffees and slid into a booth, though, she carried heavy circles under her eyes, and her lips were turned down in grief.

Mandy took the bench opposite her. "Thank you for agreeing to meet me. Steve Dulbecco said you and Irene were friends a long time."

A faint sheen of tears filmed the other woman's eyes, and her voice trembled slightly when she said, "Since junior high. We met in the marching band, and stayed in touch ever since. We always said we'd be friends until the end." She sniffled. "Neither of us thought that'd happen anytime soon, though."

Mandy stifled the urge to touch the other woman's hand, fearing she might break down at the small kindness. Instead, she sipped her coffee and kept her tone matter-of-fact. "I'm sorry to have to ask you this, but can you tell me about the night Irene was mugged?"

That brought Millie's head up. "Excuse me?"

"Steve said she called you the next day. I need to know what she told you about the attack."

"Whatever for?" Millie's confusion morphed to the beginnings of anger. "Need I remind you that Irene is dead? That she died in this very hospital? What does that have to do with her being mugged?"

Aware that the other woman's raised voice was starting to attract attention, Mandy said, "Please, I'm not trying to upset you. I'm just trying to—"

"Did she die because of the mugging?" Millie's volume climbed and she half-rose from her chair. "Did that bastard do something to her, something she didn't tell me about? Did he—"

"Sorry I'm late," a new voice said, loudly enough to interrupt.

Mandy gaped as Radcliff slid into the booth next to her, crowding her with his big body until she was forced to make room for him. He held a hand across the narrow café table. "Dr. Parker Radcliff, ma'am. I'm a member of the hospital staff on loan to the Boston Police, looking into a rash of recent muggings in this area. Thank you for meeting with us."

His air of authority and dark good looks derailed Millie in an instant.

In all honesty, Mandy couldn't blame her.

He was wearing his doctor's whites, with that stupid nickname on the breast pocket, but for the first time since her return to Boston General, Mandy didn't find it off-putting.

Instead her mind overlaid his image with that from the night before, when he'd been barefoot in worn jeans and an old sweatshirt. She might not have admitted it to herself at the time, but her fingers had itched to touch, and she'd had the mad urge to slide her hands beneath that sweatshirt to find the man beneath. Only the circumstances—and the man himself—had prevented her from making the mistake. Now, as he sat beside her and his warmth reached her, along with that special scent that was uniquely his, her stomach sent up little flares of nervous excitement, and her hormones nearly sat up and begged.

Instead of closing her eyes and inhaling him whole, though, Mandy pulled herself together and forced a glare. "I didn't think you were going to make it." Translation: *You weren't invited.*

He lifted one shoulder in an easy shrug. "I didn't want you to have to go it alone." Translation: *Don't even think of shutting me out or going off on your own.*

A low gutter of irritation took up residence beside the flare of attraction in Mandy's belly. She did have to give him some credit, though. His arrival had derailed Millie's building hysteria, which was a definite plus.

"Now." Parker glanced from Mandy to the older woman and back again. "Where were we?"

Figuring her only alternative was to cause a bigger scene than the one they'd just avoided, Mandy sighed and gave in with ill grace. "I was just asking Millie what Irene had told her about the mugging. Specifically, I was wondering if there was something she might've told her best friend that she wouldn't have told her husband or me."

When Mandy had reached Steve Dulbecco on the phone, he hadn't remembered anything more than what she already knew, but he'd admitted that he and his wife hadn't talked at length about the attack.

Mandy might've found that odd if it hadn't been for growing up with her father and stepmother, who'd lived very separate lives and often went for days without speaking more than a few words to each other. That's why she'd asked about a friend. Her stepmother's cronies had known far more about her life than her husband had cared to know.

Millie thought for a minute, then said, "Well, there was something…" She paused and colored faintly. "I'm sure Irene wouldn't want me talking to strangers about it, and under any other circumstances I wouldn't."

Figuring it was a female issue, Mandy almost asked Radcliff to take a walk. She didn't, though, partly because she knew he'd refuse and partly because she had a sneaking suspicion that he was the only reason Millie hadn't gotten up and walked out in a huff.

"Go on," she prodded gently. "We're trying to collect all the information we possibly can."

Millie considered that for a long minute before nodding. She leaned across the table and whispered, "She started going through the change early…you know what I mean?"

Radcliff nodded. "She was perimeno-pausal."

His matter-of-fact tone seemed to settle the other woman. She sat back on the padded bench and exhaled. "Yes. Well, she said that the morning after the mugging she felt nauseous. Like morning sickness, you know? She didn't want to tell Steve, because they'd wanted another baby. She wanted to keep it a surprise until she was sure." Voice soft, she said, "Was she pregnant?"

It was borderline in terms of confidentiality, but Mandy shook her head. "No, she wasn't. But thank you for telling us. The nausea was probably a reaction to the stress."

Or maybe it was a symptom, Mandy thought. There were a number of both herbal and traditional drugs that could have multiple effects, depending on the dosage and method of preparation.

"Did she tell you anything else unusual?" Radcliff pressed.

Millie thought, then shook her head. "Nothing she wouldn't have told her husband or the police." Her expression clouded. "I don't suppose I helped you much, did I?" She directed her question at Radcliff in a clear bid for reassurance, for attention.

It suddenly occurred to Mandy that if Millie had gone to school with Irene, she and Radcliff were almost the same age. A quick glance confirmed the lack of a wedding band, and the gleam of interest in the other woman's eyes.

A sudden flare of a hot irritation that could

only be jealousy surprised Mandy, and her voice was cool when she said, "Thank you for your time, Millie. We'll be in touch if we have any other questions." Translation: *Here's your hat, what's your hurry?*

Millie took the hint and stood, simpering at Radcliff. "I was on my way to Downtown Crossing, to do a little shopping. It wasn't far to come, especially if talking to you might help."

"It just might." Radcliff stood and pulled a business card holder out of the breast pocket of his lab coat, selected a card and held it out to her. "Call me anytime."

Millie's eyes gleamed. "I will." She turned and headed out of the café, and Mandy knew damn well that wiggle hadn't been in her walk when she'd arrived.

"So much for the grieving friend," she muttered. "The woman's a damned predator."

Before she could slip out of the booth Parker sat back down, trapping her. He didn't respond to her comment, instead saying, "You should thank me that we got that much out of her. More importantly, you should hope to hell I don't put you on double shifts and tell the board you've been contacting patients' families outside of hospital business."

Turning her back to the wall so she was facing him with one leg crooked up on the bench seat, holding him at a distance, she narrowed her eyes at him. "You told Aimee to page you if I went anywhere, didn't you?"

"Not just Aimee. The entire front desk staff." He didn't look the slightest bit ashamed. "Something told me you were going to go off on your own."

"I wouldn't have had to if you'd listened to me and admitted it made sense to reinterview the victims' friends and families." Mandy's knee and shin were pressed warmly against Parker's thigh, sending unwelcome shimmers of awareness through her system. She glanced down at the floor, wondering fleetingly if she could duck under the table.

"Don't even try it," he said conversationally. "You won't like what happens."

"Fine." She scowled. "So what now? You're not seriously going to put me on round-the-clock shifts, are you?"

"I should."

Something loosened inside her. "But you won't."

"Don't you care that you're in danger?"

"Of course, but I'm not going to let the fear run my life, and I'm sure as heck not hiding out when I could be helping with the investigation."

"Because of what happened to your mother." It wasn't a question.

"I'm trying not to think of it that way," she said evenly, though the memory was never far from her consciousness. "But, yes, that's part of it. If I can help Irene's kids with the closure I never got, then that's what I'm going to do."

She expected an argument. Instead Radcliff stood and looked down at her for a long moment, eyes unreadable. Then he extended his hand. "Come on."

She stood, confused. "Where are we going?"

"Stankowski ordered a full-fledged forensic autopsy of Irene's body. I'm due at the Medical Examiner's in a half hour, and I guess you're coming along for the ride."

PARKER HATED signing both of them out for a long lunch, but the E.R. was relatively quiet. Just in case, he called in two residents to cover the rest of the shift on the theory that it was better to be overstaffed than under.

Mandy was quiet during the short cab ride across town to the M.E. lab that served the entire city. He wasn't sure if she was thinking about the case or fuming that he'd elbowed in on her interview, and didn't particularly care. She was going to have to get one thing straight: whether or not either of them liked it, he was keeping close watch on her for the duration.

He knew all too well what happened to people who went rushing into dangerous situations running on emotion rather than logic.

She didn't break the silence until they were headed up the stairs to the big stone building that housed state offices on the main and second floors, the M.E.'s complex on the lower floor.

As they pushed through the doors and waited to be checked through security, she glanced at him. "Thanks for bringing me along. I know it must've seriously pained you to take me off shift."

"Don't get used to it," he said, ignoring the faint tug of disquiet at how well she knew him. "And don't expect preferential treatment once this is over."

He didn't know why he said that, and knew he sounded like an ass the moment the words left his mouth.

Her lips tightened. "Trust me, expectations are the *last* thing on my mind right now. I'm just trying to find some answers for Irene's family. Whatever else she might have been, she was my patient."

They jogged down a wide stone stairway to the M.E.'s complex, which looked both high-tech and sterile, with wide, polished hallways and neatly labeled doors.

Unable to let the conversation lie, though he knew that he absolutely, positively ought to, Parker stopped and snagged her arm, forcing her to swing around and face him.

Not sure where the impulse had come from, he gave in and touched her face, tipping her chin up so she looked him in the eyes. As it had been the night before when he'd brought her home with him, her expression was soft and vulnerable. The sight of her reached inside and twisted at him, leaving a burn of sensation he didn't recognize, one that screamed *danger*.

He let his hand fall away. "You need to learn to turn off the emotions, Mandy, and forget the losses. It's the only way you're going to survive in E.R. medicine." It wasn't what he'd meant to say, but he fell back on habit when nothing else made sense.

She looked at him for a long moment before she stepped away from him and shook her head. "I owe it to my patients not to forget them. If that means I lose some sleep, so be it. But maybe, hopefully, someday those memories will make me slow down and do one more test, ask one more question." She tilted her head. "Which makes me wonder about your strategy. How do you learn from your mistakes if you forget them the moment they're out of your life?"

"I don't make them in the first place." Parker turned away and started walking. "Come on, the M.E.'s waiting."

It turned out that he wasn't waiting at all. When Parker pushed through the door to the tile-and-steel autopsy room, he found the head pathologist, Dr. Augustus Robicheau, already at work.

The dead woman's body was laid out in the

classic position, flat on her back with her arms at her sides and her legs straight and slightly apart. Her skin was gray under the unforgiving fluorescent lights, and there were faint needle tracks in the crooks of both of her arms, where the medical professionals had taken blood and run IVs, all to no avail. Several small cuts on her body, along with the neat rows of specimen jars and evidence bags suggested that the gross external exam was well underway, but the lack of a Y-incision indicated that the pathologist had yet to get to the internal organs.

A computer sat on a rolling caddy near the autopsy table, its keyboard covered in protective plastic.

Gus Robicheau, tall and lean to the point of almost being cadaverous himself, wearing a long blue smock, yellow gloves and a face shield, looked up when they entered. "You're late."

"Sorry," Parker said. "We got hung up in an interview."

Gus transferred his attention to Mandy. "Who's this?"

"An associate of mine," Parker said

before she could answer. "Stankowski wants her in on this."

"She gonna puke?"

"Of course not. She's a—" Parker broke off when he turned and saw that Mandy had gone decidedly pale. She was staring at the body, her eyes stark holes in her head, and as he watched, she swallowed hard as though holding bile at bay.

The funk in the air was unmistakable—the smell of old death and decomp, overlain with sanitizer. That was nothing to the average doctor, though, and couldn't have accounted for Mandy's sudden pallor.

No, this was something more.

Parker cursed himself inwardly for not remembering how close this case was cutting to her mother's death. She rarely spoke of it, but from the few hints he'd gathered during their time together, he knew she'd been out with her father and they'd come home to find her mother dead in the family kitchen, surrounded by a pool of blood.

This wasn't the same, but the two cases had become linked in her mind, and he could only imagine what she was actually seeing as she looked at Irene Dulbecco's body laid out on the metal table.

"Hey," he said quietly. "You okay?"

She collected herself with a visible effort, and nodded. "Yes, I'm sorry. Please continue."

Gus gave her a long look before he nodded and returned his attention to the body. "I've done the external and taken double samples like Stankowski wanted, one set for our lab, one set for you." He didn't seem upset by the duplication of effort. "I found something interesting on the X-rays. Have a look at this." He used a pencil to tap a few computer keys and a digital X-ray popped up on the screen, showing a human skull in profile, along with the top few cervical vertebrae.

There was a small glowing spot near the occipital bone at the back of the skull.

"What is that?" Parker leaned in, noting the cylindrical shape and smooth edges of the object, which was about the size of the eraser on the end of the pathologist's pencil. "A small caliber bullet?" He frowned and glanced at Mandy. "She wasn't shot as far as we know."

"It's not a bullet."

"Then what is it?" Parker asked.

"I'll tell you in a minute if you'll let me get back to work." Gus lifted a set of electric clippers and flicked them on, effectively ending the conversation.

He bent over the body and shaved a small section of her scalp, behind her right ear. Gus clicked on a small recording device. "Removal of the hair above the site of the X-ray anomaly reveals a circular bruise, approximately one centimeter in diameter. Estimated two or three days antemortem."

He took several photographs of the bruise. Then, tipping her head to the side, he used a scalpel to cut around the area on three sides. He pulled back the resulting skin flap, muttering, "Not much in the way of tissue right here. Assuming it's not in the bone, it's gotta be just under— Aha! Gotcha."

Documenting each step with photographs, he used a pair of forceps to tease out a small metal oblong, which he dropped into a specimen jar. He capped the jar and handed it to Parker. "What do you make of this?"

"You're right, it's not a bullet." He held the container at eye level and looked at the object, which appeared completely smooth and regular, as though it was simply a metal pellet. "Not sure what it is, though." He handed the jar to Mandy. "You have any ideas? This some sort of funky homeopathic pressure point implant or something?"

She looked at it long and hard, but shook her head. "I've never seen anything like it before."

Parker set the jar with the others. "Hopefully the police techs will be able to place it."

Gus nodded. "I'll keep it in-house and see what we come up with." He straightened away from the slab. "That's it for externals." He reached for a large scalpel to begin the Y-incision. "Let's get started with—"

A siren shrilled from an overhead speaker, interrupting him.

Mandy gasped and Parker jolted. "What the hell?"

Gus glared up at the speaker and raised his voice to be heard over the din. "Fire alarm. Idiots are supposed to warn us ahead of time when they're going to pull a drill."

The pathologist stood for a minute, poised with the scalpel in his hand as if trying to decide whether to ignore the alarm and keep going with the autopsy. Finally he cursed and dropped the scalpel back into the instrument tray. "Come on." He stripped off his gloves and smock, revealing suit pants and a neatly buttoned shirt beneath. "Just in case it's not a drill."

He moved around the room, efficiently locking up the evidence and putting his computer on pass-coded standby.

There was the sound of hurried footsteps in the hallway, along with scattered shouts of inquiry. Parker caught the words *bomb threat* and *upstairs*, and his every sense went on high alert.

"Do you think this is a coincidence?" Mandy said to him under the din.

"Maybe." *Probably not*, he thought, gripping her arm and keeping her close as they followed Gus out the door.

The pathologist tapped a few keys on the coded keypad beside the door, and glanced at the other two. "The fire chief has the codes."

Which meant the body was safe from anyone without official access.

The three of them joined the flow of human traffic in the hallway. Parker kept close to Mandy, but it was difficult with the crowd teetering on the edge of hysteria.

"I smell smoke," one frazzled-looking woman said, shouting over the blare of the alarm. "Do you smell it?"

"I heard there was only sixty seconds left on the countdown," a man's voice shouted. "The place could go at any minute!"

Howls of panic greeted that announcement and the crowd surged forward, funneling into the narrow stairwell headed up. Parker lost his grip on Mandy's arm as she was jostled away from him. Seconds later, he realized he couldn't see her anymore.

"Mandy!" he shouted, cupping his hands around his mouth as fear spiked. "Mandy!"

There was no answer.

She'd disappeared.

Chapter Seven

"Help!" Mandy screamed as she was shoved into a restroom so quickly nobody around her noticed. *"Help me!"* She thrashed against her captor's hold, but the alarm drowned out her cries and he was far stronger than she.

"Shut up!" He spun her, shoved her face-first into the wall beside a paper towel dispenser and yanked her arms up behind her back.

Craning her neck, she saw hard gray eyes glittering above a surgical mask. He wore latex gloves on his hands, blue ones this time.

Heart pounding, she struggled against his grip, only half aware of the inhuman sobbing noises she was making in her terror.

Her captor shifted, holding her wrists in one hand. Pain flared in her arm and her consciousness dimmed. Everything went gray and fuzzy, and she sagged to the floor, barely conscious.

She was vaguely aware of a thud in her skull and a second prick in her arm, but it all seemed very far away for a few seconds. A voice whispered from very near her ear, "Start the clock. Seventy-two hours until you're dead."

The jolt of adrenaline cleared the mild sedative he must've hit her with first. Reality returned in a rush and she scrambled to her feet, fighting to get away from the man in the hooded sweatshirt, mask and gloves, who advanced on her, gray eyes set.

She screamed, *"Radcliff!"*

Seconds later, the bathroom door burst inward. Radcliff bared his teeth and lunged at the hooded figure. The men went down, struggling and cursing.

Radcliff must have gone for his concealed weapon and lost hold of it in the struggle, because a gun went skidding across the tiles and into a nearby bathroom stall.

"Get that!" he shouted, hanging on as the hooded man lunged to his feet and kicked Radcliff in the gut, trying to escape.

"Got it," Mandy shouted as she scrambled to the toilet stall and crouched down, fishing for the weapon Radcliff had lost. Her head spun, her arm hurt like fury and her stomach was heaving with the knowledge that her attacker had injected her with the toxin they hadn't yet been able to identify. "Don't let him get away. We need to know what's in the poison!"

Her fingers touched smooth metal. She grabbed the weapon and came up firing.

Nothing happened.

Breath sobbing in her lungs, blood a pained inferno in her veins, Mandy fumbled for the safety as the hooded man tore himself away from Radcliff and bolted for the door. She fired, blowing a chunk out of the doorjamb as he dove through. Just as Radcliff lunged in pursuit she fired again. He shouted and dove for the floor, and the bullet lodged in the door head-high.

"Stop shooting, damn it!" He surged to his feet, grabbed the gun from her and slammed through the door in pursuit. He stopped dead when the swing of the door brought a heavy cloud of smoke into the room. He reeled back, choking.

"Come on!" He beckoned for Mandy. "We've got to get out of here."

He grabbed her arm, but let go when she screamed in pain.

His eyes went hollow. "Did he get you?" When she didn't answer right away, he shook her slightly, "Mandy! Were you injected?"

She nodded, not trusting her voice.

"Where'd the syringe go?"

"I don't know," she said miserably, beginning to wheeze with the smoke. "He must've used a short-acting sedative. I remember a thud, then the injection, but none of the details."

He made a quick search. "I don't see the syringe, damn it. He must've taken it with him." He took her other arm, gently this time, and urged her toward the door. "I'm sorry, but we're going to have to make a run for it. I'm not sure what's going on out there, but I know I'd rather be outside than in here." He paused. "Can you make it?"

She nodded without speaking, afraid she'd burst into tears if she opened her mouth.

Apparently sensing that she was teetering on the edge, he slid his hand down her arm, linked his fingers with hers and squeezed. "I'm here. I've got you. Trust me."

She nodded miserably, and followed him out the door and into the smoke-filled corridor.

They were halfway up the stairs, gagging and coughing, when they met a group of fire-fighters going the other way. The team leader immediately detached two of the rescuers to get Mandy and Parker safely outside.

Before he went, Parker grabbed the team leader's arm. "There may be a man down there. He's wearing a hooded sweatshirt and dark jeans, and may have gloves or a mask on. He's dangerous, and he's wanted by the police. Be careful with him, but whatever you do, don't let him get away!"

Then they were being hustled outside, into the blessed fresh air. Mandy collapsed to the curb on the opposite side of the street from the smoke-filled building. There was smoke but no fire. She'd heard someone say there had been six smoke bombs set to go off si-multaneously in different parts of the building, but the information had only regis-tered on the surface of her brain.

She was vaguely aware of fire trucks and

police cars in the road, and groups of people gathered on either side of the road, but most of her attention was focused inward, at the changes she could feel beginning inside her body.

Her arm was throbbing and her hands and feet tingled, though she didn't know if the tingling was from the injection or fear. Ditto the nausea that clamped her belly, making her want to retch, and the shivers that racked her body. Seventy-two hours, he'd said. She had three days until she wound up stretched out on a slab like Irene Dulbecco.

"Stankowski assigned us a car to get you to Boston General," Radcliff said, coming up beside her and crouching down to touch her shoulder in the gentlest of squeezes. "It would've been best to test what was in the syringe, but if we take blood now, the toxin shouldn't have broken down into metabolites. We should be able to identify it, and figure out how to treat it…" He trailed off. "Aw, hell. Come here." He pulled her to her feet, wrapped his arms around her and hung on. "I'm sorry, Mandy. I'm so damned sorry."

That was when Mandy burst into tears, because if Radcliff was being nice to her, it had to be real.

PARKER PACED outside Exam One while an officer took Mandy's statement and clothes, and took pictures of the injection sites on her arm.

He cursed himself with every breath, knowing it was his fault she'd been there to be attacked. He should've left her at the hospital that morning, or better yet back at his place. Hell, he should've put her on a plane to L.A. and call for her father to meet her at the airport. The esteemed Dr. Sparks, surgeon to half of Hollywood and head of more medical boards than he could count, might not think much of his daughter dating an old hack E.R. doc who'd never aspired beyond BoGen, but he'd damn well have stepped in if he'd known she was in danger.

Now it was too late; the countdown had begun. They had three days to figure out what the bastard was using and how to counteract it.

"How is she?" Stankowski said, coming up beside him and leaning against a nearby wall.

"She's miserable," Parker snapped. "How would you be if you'd just been injected with a ticking time bomb?" Then he cursed and stopped pacing. "Sorry. I'm angry."

"I am, too," the detective said quietly. "And I'm going to get this bastard, Parker. I swear it."

But he didn't promise he could do it in seventy-two hours.

Footsteps clicked in the hallway, and Parker looked up to find one of his most trusted radiologists approaching fast.

She nodded before he could even ask the question. "You were right. There's a small anomaly at the base of her skull."

Parker cursed, but couldn't quell the flare of triumph. "Get it out ASAP and give it to the detective here." He turned to Stankowski. "I think they're tracking devices—GPS maybe, or something even more sophisticated. Can your people backtrack the signal?"

"We'll do our best." Stankowski grabbed the wall phone, dialed for an outside line and rapped out an order for one of his team members to pick up the other small metal pellet from Dr. Robicheau. When he hung up, he nodded. "They're on it. As soon as the other one is out of Mandy, I'll take it to them myself."

"Did they get anything off that disk Mandy found?"

The detective shook his head. "They're still working on it, but it's in tough shape. It is— or was—a recordable audio disk for one of those miniature playback machines, but all they're getting off it so far is garbage. They'll be better off focusing on these transmitters— if that's what they are. At least we're positive they're part of the case. For all we know, the disk is just trash someone threw out in one of those Dumpsters." Stankowski paused for a minute, and then glanced at the doorway to Exam One. "I assume you're going to admit her for the duration?"

"No," Parker said without hesitation. "She's coming with me. I guarantee that she'll want to remain part of the investigation."

Stank frowned. "Wouldn't she be safer here?"

"Maybe," Parker said. "Probably, but it's not fair. If you potentially had three days left and you were going to feel okay for at least two of them, would you want to spend that time in the hospital?"

"No, but you could start her on some prophylactic drugs, couldn't you?"

"What drugs do you suggest?" Parker spread his hands. "We don't have a clue what killed Julian George and Irene Dulbecco, and presumably killed Missy Prieta. I can treat the symptoms, sure, but don't you get it? I can't do a damned thing to stop this until we figure out what the hell it is!" Parker was shouting by the time he finished, and when he fell silent, he was aware that several nearby staffers were staring at him.

He could only imagine what the rumor mill would have to say about him losing his cool. He wasn't sure he cared, though. He had far more important things to worry about.

The door to Exam One swung open and the female officer stepped out, carrying a large bag that no doubt contained Mandy's clothes and whatever other evidence had been collected. The officer nodded to Parker and Stankowski. "You can go in now. I'll get this stuff over to forensics."

"You go," Parker told the detective. "She

gave me the combo to her locker in the staff lounge. I'm going to get her spare clothes."

It was an escape and he damn well knew it, but he just couldn't bring himself to see Mandy as a patient. That was why he'd elected not to pull rank and see to her care himself, and why he lingered in the staff lounge long after he'd grabbed the small overnight bag from her locker.

She wasn't a patient, damn it. She was—

Parker couldn't complete the train of thought, because he didn't know what she was to him anymore. He did know one thing, though. She wasn't anyone's victim.

He wouldn't let her be.

MANDY WINCED against the tug when Dr. Gina Stuart, the E.R.'s head attending, pulled the last of the stitches tight behind her ear.

"There you go. Good as new," Gina announced, but her eyes remained dark and worried.

"Radcliff told you what happened, didn't he?" Mandy asked.

Gina hesitated, then nodded. "He told a few of us, only the ones he needed to get the samples rushed, and so we could put our heads together on some sort of supportive therapy for you."

Mandy held still as the other woman pressed a bandage over the small incision she'd made to remove the metal pellet from her head. And how creepy was that? She had to suppress another shudder at the thought of carrying around an implant, like she'd been the victim of an alien abduction or something.

Somehow it was easier to think about that than about the toxins flooding her bloodstream. The implant could be—and had been— removed and given to Stankowski for analysis.

The toxins were still an open question. Maybe the analysis of her blood samples would reveal something useful. Then again, maybe not, which left her with a ticking clock in her body, and no great faith that the mystery could be solved in time.

At the thought, tears filmed her vision.

"Take this," Gina said briskly, pressing an unmarked case into her hands. The white plastic container was approximately the size and shape of a lunch box, with a handle and clasps at the top. It was the sort of thing they used to transport samples or drugs short distances from building to building, when they didn't want to attract too much attention on the street.

"What's in it?"

"A little bit of everything." Gina popped the top and showed her a wide range of single-dose syringes and foil packets. She indicated a folded sheet of paper. "There's a list of what in here, and what doses. Dr. Radcliff picked out most of it."

It took Mandy a minute to catch on. Then she straightened on the exam room bed and pulled the too-short robe down to cover the tops of her thighs. "He's not putting me under observation?"

"Yes and no," his voice said unexpectedly from the doorway. He pushed through, carrying her overnight bag, which he tossed on the bed beside her. "You'll be under my observation for the duration." He paused. "Unless of course you'd rather spend the next three days in here. If so, I'll get you a private room and—"

"No," she interrupted quickly, dipping into the bag for her jeans, which she pulled on beneath the robe without regard for modesty. "Let's go."

Sudden adrenaline buzzed through her veins, clearing some of the fog that had surrounded her since they'd arrived at the hospital and she'd found her role shifting from her normal guise of doctor to the uncomfortable position of being a patient in her own hospital. As the fog burned away, she felt a new determination take root, a new focus.

She had three days to solve the case and save her own life.

ONCE THEY WERE in a cab, headed away from Boston General, Parker gave the driver Mandy's home address.

At her questioning look, he shrugged. "I figured you'd want to get a few things. I cleared it with Stankowski. He says the drive-bys still haven't indicated any activity at your place, and the apartment manager got the locks changed."

"Then I can stay there if I want?" she asked, glancing over at him.

He tried to interpret her expression, but failed. It seemed as though she'd developed a cool facade of her own, one he couldn't read, and though he'd once wished she could be more detached and less emotional about her patients and her life, now he found himself discomfited by the change.

"I suppose you could," he said slowly. "But I'd really prefer that you come home with me."

He halfway expected her to ask him why. The Mandy he'd known before—younger, untried and idealistic and prone to wearing her heart on her sleeve—would've taken the opportunity to make him declare himself one way or the other. Did he want her at his place because he wanted her around and wanted to comfort her, or was it merely a case of safety and expedience?

The hell of it was that he wasn't sure of the answer anymore. The discipline he depended on to keep him on track had blurred to something else over the past few hours—or maybe the past few days—and he wasn't sure where his boundaries fell anymore.

She didn't ask why, though. She simply nodded and looked out the window of the cab as the driver pulled up in front of her apartment building. "Okay."

Her acquiescence surprised him. Even more surprising, he found he was faintly disappointed, as though a part of him had wanted the question, and the argument it was sure to bring.

The realization stirred him up and had him brooding as he followed her up the steps to her building, where she buzzed the apartment manager and got a set of keys to the new locks. It wasn't until they reached the hallway outside her fourth-floor apartment that he touched her arm to stop her, and turn her so they were face-to-face.

He looked down at her, seeing the stress and fear behind the calm mask she was wearing like a shield.

"Hey," he said, brushing a finger across her cheek where a faint bruise touched her fair skin. "I'm here for you, okay? I promise I'm not going anywhere until—" He broke off because he'd been about to say *until this is over,* but that sounded far too final, too dismal. Instead he said, "Don't be afraid to lean on me. I'm here for the duration."

She smiled crookedly, but the expression didn't seem to reach her eyes. "Thanks. I'll keep that in mind."

Then she turned away, leaving him feeling as though he'd wanted more just then...but he'd be damned if he knew what that might be. He should be satisfied with where they were at, he knew. He'd done the right thing in getting her out of the hospital, he'd called in all the favors he could think of and put a team of Boston General's top researchers and doctors on a think tank dedicated to testing the samples they'd collected from the mugging victims, and he was going to drive himself the next seventy-two hours straight if that was what it took to figure out how to save her. It was all that anyone could ask,

Oddly enough, though, as he followed her through the door into her apartment, he wasn't sure that was enough for him.

Then Mandy stopped dead.

"What is it?" Every muscle in Parker's body tensed for battle and he moved quickly in front of her.

On the floor just inside the door lay a plain sheet of paper, folded in half.

"We shouldn't touch it," Mandy said. "It could be important."

"Or it could be a menu for a new restaurant around the block," Parker said, but didn't argue her point. "You have any gloves around here?" When she shook her head, he improvised, removing a pen from his inner pocket and crouching down to flip the sheet over and tease it open without putting his fingerprints on it.

It turned out that the piece of paper wasn't folded, after all; it had been ripped in half. There was a single line of text in handwritten in bold, slashing pen strokes: THE ANTIDOTE FOR THE DISK. MEET ME AT—

The rest was gone, torn away.

"Where's the other half?" Mandy demanded. She looked around, but there was no sign of the other piece having been stuck under her door. "Where is it?" Her voice rose, growing shrill.

"I don't know." Parker rose to his feet and caught her hands, feeling the first beat of optimism. "But, Mandy, think about it. This means there is an antidote."

The only thing for them to do now was find it, and the note told them exactly where to start.

With the disk.

Chapter Eight

The next two hours were filled with another round of police questions and crime scene analysis, and even though Stankowski did his best to minimize the invasion, Mandy's head was pounding by the time she and Parker were cleared to leave.

Her heart hurt, too. Logically she knew the worst part had been the attack at the M.E. building, but there was something profoundly disturbing about watching the cops rummage around in her apartment. Stankowski had insisted on the search even though she'd protested that the note had been slipped under the door.

Given that his techs had positively identified the metal pellet extracted from her neck as a small but highly powerful transmitter, and were working on determining exactly what information it was designed to transmit, she hadn't argued against the search, but it had bothered her nonetheless.

Having the cops in there had made her apartment seem even more Spartan somehow, and the unpacked boxes had loomed large in her vision. Even her herbs had looked wilted and unloved, giving her pinches of guilt.

Over it all had hovered the specter of the countdown and the million-dollar question: What was the antidote mentioned in the note, and where could they get their hands on it?

Mandy knew she should be raring to launch into the search, but found herself fading fast. By the time the police left, she was just about done in. She grabbed a bunch of clothes at random and stuffed them in the leather duffel she used as a suitcase. Exhaustion dragged at her arms and legs, making her feel as though she were moving in slow motion, dragging herself through sludge instead of air.

When she joined Parker—and yes, in the midst of everything that was going on, he'd gone from "Radcliff" to "Parker" in her head, whether either of them liked it or not—in the main room, she tried to keep the quiver out of her voice when she said, "I don't feel well. I'm tired and nauseous, and it's like I'm constantly on the verge of tears. I think it's starting already."

"No, you're on the brink of exhaustion and you haven't eaten since last night," he said bluntly. "Let's get out of here. We'll grab some takeout and head home. You can sleep while I follow up on the tests and make some calls."

"We should both be working on the case," she argued, irritation flaring despite—or perhaps because of—her fatigue. "God knows I've got some serious personal motivation now. As in, I'm not going to see next week if we don't figure out what's inside me and how to counteract it."

Even as she said the words, she realized they were a plea for sympathy, a demand that he acknowledge what she was going through, maybe even tell her he was sorry, that he'd miss her.

Damn it, she thought. She'd fallen right back onto old patterns, asking him for attention, for emotions she knew he couldn't give.

Sure enough, he said simply, "You can't help me when you're this tired. Eat something, turn it off for a few hours and then you'll be useful."

Oddly, though, instead of hurting her or ticking her off, his words steadied her. She found herself nodding agreement. "Gotcha."

She locked the door to her apartment and tried not to think that it could be the last time she saw the place. She followed Parker out to street level, and was surprised to see that dusk was falling. Where had the day gone? A quick check of her watch showed that she was down to sixty-seven hours, give or take.

She told herself Parker was crazy if he thought she was going to waste five or six of those hours sleeping. She was still thinking that once they were in a cab, headed for the Chinese restaurant where he'd phoned in an order.

Before they'd gone two blocks, she'd fallen asleep, leaning against his shoulder.

PARKER WORKED through the night, refusing to feel the fatigue that tried to drag him down, or the frustration that threatened to distract him from his main objective: figuring out what the hell had been in that syringe, where it had come from, and who had the antidote. Problem was, there were too many angles to come at the questions, and it was impossible to tell which one would be the most valuable.

By 2:00 a.m., he was sitting on the wide sofa in the main room with his laptop on the coffee table, eating cold lo-mein straight from the carton and drinking mug after mug of tea, because the coffee had started burning a hole in his gut. He didn't give any credit to the quick suspicion that the pain had come from another source entirely, one who looked like a beach bunny and thought that herbs could replace real medicine, but had lodged herself somewhere inside him and threatened to take over his better sense.

Instead of thinking about such things, he bent to his work, determined to heal her. Never mind that he rarely brought anything but administrative work home, and his famed "leave each patient at the door to the exam room" motto had clearly taken a flying leap...he was a doctor, damn it; this was his job.

Emotion didn't have anything to do with it. He went over all his notes for what felt like the thousandth time, unable to escape the feeling that the answer was right in front of him.

Logically the symptoms didn't add up. The sudden onset and degree of pain and its widespread nature suggested a few conditions. Sepsis was one option; a generalized infection could inflame neurons throughout the body, making the skin acutely sensitive to pressure. That didn't work as a diagnosis, though, because neither Irene Dulbecco nor Julian George had shown the elevated white blood cell count indicative of an infection.

Yet they'd both died in terrible pain, just as Mandy might if he didn't come up with the medical equivalent of pulling a rabbit out of a hat, and Stankowski and his people didn't manage to come up with some theories to go with the scant evidence they'd managed to collect so far.

Parker trusted Stank—he was a good cop, and didn't let emotion get in the way of his job. But he wasn't a miracle worker, either. What were the odds the detective could crack the case in less than three days when he'd been working on it for weeks now?

The thought—and the lack of any real answers—drove Parker to his feet. He considered pacing a pointless waste of time and energy, so he never bothered. Instead he usually burned off his frustrations in the weight room downstairs.

Since he didn't want to be downstairs and zoned out if Mandy needed him, he opted for another form of therapy, heading for the kitchen and filling a small copper watering can, then adding a few granules of fertilizer.

Even before he'd crossed to the nearest hanging pot, where a spider plant dangled runners and starbursts of rootless offspring, he felt himself relaxing slightly.

The plants had been the decorator's idea; she'd said he needed something alive in the town house. Since he'd been sleeping with her at the time, he'd let her have her way.

The decorator hadn't lasted long—none of his liaisons did, thanks to his careful choices—but oddly enough the plants had stuck. He thought feng shui was a crock, but had to admit that the greenery was pleasant. He hadn't gone so far as to talk to the things, but he watered them precisely on schedule and had even added a row of African violets in the front room, for a bit of texture and color.

From the spider plant in the kitchen he moved out into the main room, checking dampness with his forefinger and adding as needed—a little more for the begonias near the window, less for the cactus, which was a favorite of his because it looked spiky and fierce but felt soft to the touch.

As he moved around the room, hardly even aware that he was humming softly, his mind continued to work.

The lab hadn't been able to find any of the testable poisons in Mandy's blood, and all of her clinicals were within normal limits, just like the two patients before her. The lack of a detectable poison could mean it was cleared almost immediately from the blood, taking up residence in specific organs or tissues.

That possibility had some potential, Parker mused. A number of companies were working on targeting vectors that could help deliver a drug directly to the site of action, thus decreasing overall toxicities and side effects. What if—

"Parker?"

He spun at the sound of his name, and found Mandy standing halfway up the stairs, sleepy-eyed and pale, but with a light in her eyes that made his heart stutter in his chest.

She wore a pale blue T-shirt and dark blue bike shorts that should've looked practical rather than sexy but somehow managed both, nearly causing Parker to dump the last half-gallon of water on the floor.

Cautiously he set the watering can aside. "You should get some more sleep. You need the rest."

"Stop trying to tell me what I need and what I should be doing," she said, but there was no rancor in the words. Just a statement of fact. She continued down the stairs, and though part of Parker told him to move forward—or away—he stayed rooted to the spot. When she reached him, she pulled back one of the cap sleeves of her T-shirt, baring her upper arm and shoulder. "Look."

There was a pinprick red rash, about the size of a half-dollar, high on her shoulder.

"Irene had a patch on her thigh," she said. "She assumed it was road rash from the mugging. It wasn't. It was an injection site reaction."

Parker cursed and felt something snap tight within him. It wasn't until he saw that rash, that proof of contamination, that it hit him, really hit him.

She was dying in front of his eyes.

"Mandy," he began, then fell silent because he didn't know what to say. He hadn't been the man she'd needed four years ago and he hadn't treated her well, but some piece of him had felt a measure of satisfaction knowing that she was out there, living her life, far happier than she would've been if he'd tried to keep her.

In a few short days, he wouldn't even have that cold comfort.

"I know," she said. She looked away from him as though not wanting him to see the sheen of tears in her eyes. "This really, really stinks. The thing is, crying and complaining about the unfairness of it all isn't going to change anything. Unless we come up with a miracle, I have a little over sixty hours left." She squared her shoulders as though talking herself into being brave, and faced him, letting him see the tears in her eyes, along with something else.

Something that looked an awful lot like an invitation.

"Don't do anything you'll regret," he said, though he wasn't sure which one of them he was trying to warn off. "We could still beat this thing. We could still—"

"Or we might not," she said, interrupting him. "And if we don't, the only thing I'll regret is not taking this chance right now." She took a deep breath, as though gathering her courage, and said, "Even if we weren't in this together, I think you'd be the man I'd track down for one last fling, Parker. We couldn't make the emotional stuff work out between us back then, and I doubt we could manage it now, but the sex was nothing short of fantastic. I don't know about you, but I haven't done any better in the years since."

Though it wasn't a question, Parker found himself shaking his head. "No. Me, neither."

He'd had lovers since, but none like her. None that had tempted him to want more, despite all the other stuff being a bad match.

"Then we have tonight and tomorrow night," she said with quiet dignity. "For tonight, at least, this is what I want. I want you, Parker. I want us back, at least for a few hours."

He felt a strange pressure in his chest, a ripping, tearing pain that quickly faded to a dull throb. He looked away for a second, unable to find his voice when all he wanted to do was curse the unfairness, the wrongness of what had happened to her, what he'd let happen. But she didn't need the anger from him right now, he knew. She needed more than he would usually be able to give, more than he'd ever given before.

And by damn he was going to find a way to give it to her.

He stepped into her, framed her face in his hands and looked into her eyes, willing her to believe the truth of it when he said, "If that's what you want, then you've got it. For tonight and tomorrow night, I'm yours."

Then he kissed her.

MANDY EXPECTED—was looking forward to—the commanding sexuality she remembered from before, a rush of heat and flame that would help her forget herself for a few precious, necessary hours.

Instead she found a level of tenderness that both melted and unnerved her.

Parker's kiss began with a whisper and a sigh, and when she parted her lips on a murmur of pleasure, he moved in closer and aligned himself with her, mouth to mouth, tongue to tongue, testing and touching rather than taking, asking rather than demanding.

The gentleness was a surprise, and something of a danger, because it made her wish for impossible things. As his lips cruised across hers, though, she found part of what she'd been looking for. She found oblivion.

The kiss spun out slowly, softly, coating her in an insulating warmth that made her feel that they were the only two people in existence, that the universe began and ended where their tongues touched.

His hands slid across the skin of her waist and lower back, beneath the gym shirt she'd slept in, which suddenly felt as though it were made of the softest silk, the sexiest lace. Her bike shorts chafed between her legs, rubbing at the aching flesh that demanded release. Demanded him.

Heat flared through her, whipping around her core and settling there in a fiery response that felt so blessedly normal amidst the craziness of the past few days that she almost wept with the sensation. Instead of crying, though, she focused on making him feel the same sort of burn, the same need.

Somewhere deep inside her, she acknowledged a basic truth. She wanted Parker to miss her when she was gone, just as she'd missed him over the past four years.

She poured herself into the kiss, into the moment, and was rewarded by his hum of pleasure when they slid deeper into the kiss. Together.

He broke the kiss and looked at her, really looked at her, his cobalt-blue eyes focused intently, making her feel as though she was the only thing that mattered to him just then. He slid his hand up her arm, pushing her short sleeve up over the pinprick rash that had been the final confirmation, the final blow that might've shattered her resolve, but instead had sent her downstairs in search of what she wanted. What she needed.

He touched his lips to the spot, making the skin there burn even hotter than before. Then he looked at her once again, and said simply, "I'm yours. You're mine."

"For tonight," she agreed, knowing that was why he'd been able to drop his natural barriers as far as he had, and let her inside. If there had been any threat of a future together, she never would've gotten this far. They never would've been together, as they were together now.

He might not be able to do a lifetime of commitment, but he could—and would— give her the next sixty hours.

"Let's go upstairs." He slid his hand down her arm and linked his fingers with hers in achingly simple intimacy.

When she nodded, he led her back the way she'd come. She half expected them to wind up in the guest room that had become hers, for a few days at least. Instead he led her to the master suite. His space. His privacy.

Telling herself not to make the gesture into more than it actually was, Mandy followed him into the bedroom. He kept the bedroom lamps off, but light spilled in from the hallway, and from a night-light in the master bath, creating a shadowy illumination that was almost painfully romantic.

She knew this wasn't about romance at all, but her heart shuddered in her chest when he turned to face her and lifted her hand, then kissed her inner wrist, where the blood pulsed just beneath her skin.

The dim light shadowed his face, but she could see his eyes, which gleamed with heat and something that she thought might be tenderness. The presence of that emotion, which she'd asked for from him before and been denied, only served to remind her of the situation and the fleeting futility of it all, but she forced herself to shove the thought aside and focus on that moment.

She wanted this, damn it. She'd missed this, and if she could pick one set of sensations to take with her, it would be this. It would be him, and what she felt when she was with him.

Recognizing that simple truth when nothing else was simple, she withdrew her hand from his and pulled her T-shirt off, slowly and with quiet dignity, but without preamble. She shimmied out of her bike shorts and panties next, until she was standing there, in the center of his bedroom, clothed in nothing but shadows while he remained fully dressed.

"Take me to bed," she said. "Now."

He stared at her for a long moment before the corner of his mouth kicked up faintly. "Far be it from me to go against a doctor's orders."

Then he took her in his arms, lifting her as though she weighed nothing, and carried her to the bed.

He set her down gently, as though she were fragile and precious, and followed her down and stretched out alongside her, still fully clothed. They pressed close, kissing and touching, and when she slid her leg up his and hooked her calf around his hips, baring herself to his touch, the rasp of his pants fabric against the sensitive skin of her inner thigh was brutally erotic.

She murmured and arched against him, moaning when his fingers found her, touching and teasing her, bringing her blood to a slow, insistent burn. That burn brought frustration when she couldn't touch him in return, and she tugged at his shirt, sliding her hands beneath so she could go to work on his jeans.

"You're wearing too many clothes," she said, caught between a groan and a laugh when her fingers slipped on the button of his jeans. "And please tell me you have a condom. Preferably more than one."

He chuckled and drew her in for a long kiss, where tenderness was edged with growing passion. "Be right back."

The mattress dipped under his weight and then sprang back when he stood. She watched him undress, loving the play of light and dark across his skin. When he was fully naked, and she saw him standing proud and erect for her, her heart hitched faintly in her chest and the burn of tears gathered at the back of her eyes. She wasn't feeling sadness, though, or regret. It was a kick of anger that he hadn't wanted to share this with her before, that he'd been too selfish to compromise, too caught up in himself to see how good they could be together.

Or maybe he'd seen it, and it hadn't been

enough for him, she thought on a bite of temper, and the thought made her want to brand herself onto his soul. That was why, when he returned to the bed and lay beside her once more, facing her and looking into her eyes, she cupped his face in her hands and touched her lips to his. "Remember me," she whispered. "Remember this."

Surprising her, he caught her wrists in his hands and deepened the kiss until she felt as though he'd reached inside her, and she into him. "I do," he said simply. "I will."

And with those words, so like the marriage vows she'd probably never exchange with another in her lifetime, he rolled over and settled himself atop her, their bodies fitting together so exquisitely, the sensation was almost painful in its intensity.

He looked down at her, into her, and everything else ceased to exist. The world became him, nothing but him, as she wrapped her legs around his hips and angled herself so his latex-sheathed length was poised for entry.

They paused there for a second, for an eternity, staring into each other's eyes. Then slowly, inch by filling inch, he eased inside her, stretching her, pressing on neurons that had been long dormant, but now flared to blazing life.

Mandy moaned and moved restlessly against him, wanting the flash and flame, wanting all of him, wanting the madness only he could bring her.

He stayed slow, though, until he was fully inside her. Then he paused once again, making her acutely conscious of his good, solid weight, and how the scent of their love-making drenched her senses. She burrowed her face into the side of his neck, pressing her cheek against him as tears threatened, as panic threatened with the realization that she might never again feel this way.

"Hush, sweetheart," he said, his voice a low rumble in his chest. "I've got you. Hang on to me and everything will be okay."

It was an empty promise, perhaps, but it was exactly what she needed. Nodding against his neck, she wrapped her arms around him, tightened her legs around him, and held on for all that she was worth as he began to move.

He thrust strongly, rhythmically, with all

the control that might be frustrating in daily life, but became an asset in the bedroom, allowing him to draw out her pleasure, sending her spiraling ever upward.

Abandoning her fears and resentments to the joy of the moment, Mandy threw her head back and held on. He quickened the tempo, gripping her hips and driving into her, deeper and deeper until he touched her core, touched the center of her being, where the need and heat had coiled, hard and hot. He groaned as he rocked against her, bowing his head until his hair brushed against her cheek and collarbone, soft in comparison to the hardness everywhere else, and the excitement within her.

The first orgasm caught her almost unawares, rising up and slapping through her thin layer of self-control, leaving her scrambling to catch up with her own body as she bowed beneath him and cried out.

Sensation piled atop sensation when he didn't stop, didn't slow, driving her immediately up to another, sharper orgasm that wrung a groan out of her as her inner muscles clamped down, pulsing against his hard length until he finally cut loose with a shout, coming within her, clamping his arms around her and holding on until she could barely breathe. But she didn't need to breathe, didn't need to think, didn't need to do anything but hold onto Parker's solid body, which anchored her against the storm of sensation within.

Murmuring half-heard endearments to each other, they clung as the waves passed and they could lie there, still joined, breathing in unison. There was no need for conversation, for a postmortem, each of them knew why they were there and how much it had meant—or hadn't meant—in future terms.

Knowing it, Mandy didn't hesitate when he rolled off her and onto his side. She took his hand, wrapped it around her waist and snuggled up against him, so they were pressed together back-to-front, sweat cooling them together.

They lay like that, unspeaking in the darkness, with no words necessary. After a while, Parker's rhythmical breathing indicated he'd fallen asleep, which was good, because she wasn't the only one who'd been short on rest.

The few hours she'd gotten—and the sex—had charged her batteries, though, and she found herself too revved to doze. Maybe it was the unexpected intimacy she'd found in his arms, maybe the specter of a giant countdown hanging over her. Either way, she found herself driven out of the warm cocoon of bedclothes and man.

In the guest room she rummaged through the duffel she'd thrown together back at her apartment, and changed into a pair of jeans and heavy socks, along with a turtleneck and a sweatshirt from a long-ago medical convention down in Florida, which she, Kim and a handful of other Wannabes had attended more for the beaches and party atmosphere than the actual meeting.

The thought of her friends brought a stab of renewed fear and remorse to go with the residual hum of good sex, reminding her that it wasn't just Parker and what they might've had that she would be leaving behind if she died, it was everything else: Kim and the Wannabes, her patients, even her father and stepfamily. She might not be close to them, but that didn't mean she ever in a million years wanted to cause them the pain of losing a daughter the way she'd lost her mother.

With the thought came a new sense of resolution. *It's not over yet,* she told herself, drawing a measure of strength from the inner words. She scratched absently at the rash on her arm, but forced herself to stop when she realized what she was doing.

Then she froze, staring at the rash.

What if, she thought as her heart started drumming with excitement, *the trick we're missing isn't in the poison at all?*

What if it was in the delivery?

PARKER WOKE well before the late winter dawn, which was totally, utterly normal for him. What wasn't normal was the faint sting of disappointment he felt when he realized Mandy wasn't there, and the subsequent flush of discomfort when he remembered how far things had gone the night before.

It wasn't the physical aspect that had him staying in the shower longer than usual, trying to figure out his next move. Sex was sex, after all, and he'd had enough positive feedback over the years to know he was pretty good at it. More importantly, it had never been a question that he and Mandy were good together. Heck, they were beyond good, and that was the problem, because he'd gotten in way deeper than he'd meant to the night before, way deeper than he ever had before, even with his ex-wife, who he'd been crazy about when they married.

But, as she'd pointed out too many times to count, being crazy about someone wasn't the same as loving them. Crazy was something you could step away from, love wasn't. Love was all about emotion, all about setting aside logic and letting go.

It was about forever.

Mandy might not have forever, though. Unless they pulled off a miracle, she had the next two days and that was it. If having him close to her, both physically and emotionally, for that time would help, then that's what he was going to do.

Ignoring the faint warning chime in the back of his brain, he headed downstairs expecting to find her in the kitchen, showered and powering up with a cup of coffee.

He found her in the living room with

papers strewn around her. She was muttering to herself as he came into the room, and when he cleared his throat, she looked up quickly, her eyes wild. "I think he's using nanotechnology to send the toxin particles into the organs, getting them out of the bloodstream as quickly as possible. Question is—where is he sending them and how can we block it?"

Chapter Nine

Driven by the excitement of a testable hypothesis, Mandy and Parker headed straight to Boston General and started culling the blood samples for synthetic oil particles. Once they had them, mass spectrometry gave them a chemical breakdown of the oil. By nine o'clock that morning, they had their delivery system. They even had a brand name: Dynastin 402.

Unfortunately that wasn't enough to tell them how to clear the toxin from Mandy's blood, leaving them so close, yet so far from the answer.

Refusing to give up, she kept cranking while Parker brought Stankowski up to speed.

"Let me get this straight." The detective frowned at his notes. "The rash and the lack of toxins in the blood samples made you look at oil-based drug delivery systems called nanoparticles. These things can cause rashes at the site of injection. I get that. What I don't get is why your blood tests didn't find them in the first place. The whole 'nano' thing makes me think of Verne's *Incredible Journey*, when they shrank that spaceship thing and injected it into a person."

"It's sort of like that," Parker said, "only not really. Nanoparticles aren't robots, but you're right that they're really small—the technical term is nanoscale. They're basically very small spheres made of several layers. The inner layer, the core, is where the drug— or in this case, the poison—is loaded. It's surrounded by an outer shell of oil."

Stankowski nodded. "This Dynastin 402 you found in Mandy's blood sample from yesterday."

"Exactly. One end of the Dynastin molecule likes to interact with aqueous solutions—like blood plasma—and one end is repelled by those same solutions, so Dynastin molecules automatically self-assemble into tiny little spheres, with one end pointing toward the plasma and the other end protected inside the sphere. Mix it with your drug of choice and then expose it to an aqueous environment, and poof! Self-assembling, drug-loaded nanoparticles."

Stankowski didn't seem convinced. "If there are all these little balls floating around in the blood, why didn't they show up when we tested the other samples?"

"Because making the nanoparticles is only half the battle. You've also got to target them so they release the drug at the proper spot. That's why scientists are so hot on the technology—in theory, nanoparticles should be able to deliver a drug directly to the action site—a tumor, for example—meaning that treatment dosages can be lower and more specific. Less toxicity for chemotherapy, that sort of thing. They do it by attaching recognition molecules to the end of the Dynastin, so they end up on the outside of the particle. Then the particles float around in the bloodstream until they bump up against the cell type they're designed to recognize, and they dump their drug load."

"You said in theory," Stankowski put in. "These things aren't real yet?"

"They're real enough," Parker said. "There's still some optimization necessary before they're the drug agent of choice, but they're definitely out there."

Mandy half-listened to the conversation while she waited for the printout results of her latest Mass Spec run, which she was hoping would tell them which targeting sequence was being used. They were sitting in a computer room off the second floor lab complex above the E.R. Being back at the hospital felt strange for some reason, as though she didn't fit there anymore. She wasn't sure if it was her being off-shift, the investigation, or what had happened between her and Parker the night before, but she felt as though something had shifted inside her.

She felt as though she didn't belong at Boston General anymore. But if that was the case, where *did* she belong?

Before she could come up with an answer for that question, the MS results popped up on her computer screen. When she saw that she'd actually gotten an answer, she jolted in surprise. When she saw the result, she hissed with satisfaction. "Gotcha, you bastard."

The men instantly crowded around her. "You got the targeting sequence?" Parker demanded.

He reached to grab the printout, but she held it away. "It looks like he got his hands on one of the newer generations, the kind that're programmed to congregate at the peripheral nerve bundles."

Which explained the pain symptoms, she thought with a shiver.

"Does knowing that help?" Stankowski asked quickly.

"It might," Mandy said, turning for a nearby computer, only to find Parker there ahead of her, pounding away at the keyboard. "Anyone local been working on neurotargeting?"

He scanned the list of articles offered through the linked MedLine databases. "I don't see any—wait. Here's one." He clicked on the link and pulled up an abstract that summarized the full paper. He scrolled down to the bottom, where the university and company affiliations of each of the authors were listed. "UniVax Pharmaceuticals is working on a system, but it looks like they've hit some glitches in the Phase II trials." He glanced at her. "They're reporting 'unacceptable side effects.' What do you want to bet that includes systemic pain?"

And death. He didn't say the words, but he didn't have to. They all knew what was at stake.

She nodded. "Do you know anyone over there we could talk to?"

He grimaced, "I know *of* the CEO more than I know her personally. Arabella Cuthbert aka Cutthroat Cuthbert. She doesn't have a warm and fuzzy reputation."

Mandy winced. "Coming from Dr. Detachment himself, that's saying a lot."

"I'll call in a warrant," Stankowski said, reaching for the phone.

"Make it as broad as you can," Parker instructed. "We'll want to get a look at their access logs, so we know exactly who can and has put their hands on the targeting sequence in the past few months. We'll also want to get a look at those Phase II reports and see what sort of side effects they were having."

As he spoke, Parker pushed away from the computer and stood, and Mandy was struck afresh by how tall he was, how broad and commanding, seeming to fill any room he walked into. That reminded her of the night before, bringing a faint wash of heat, a faint tug of wistfulness when she wondered if he regretted having missed the past four years with her, or if he was, on some deeply buried level, relieved to know their affair had a definite endpoint this time. A permanent one.

Don't think that way, she chided herself, knowing she was projecting her own fears onto Parker, who had been nothing but kind and supportive all morning. Which, she admitted privately, was part of the problem. His attentiveness only served to underscore the ticking clock, because she knew damn well he'd never have acted that way under normal circumstances.

"Got it," Stankowski said, interrupting her thoughts. He hung up the phone with a decisive click. "There's definitely some pressure coming down from above, because that's about the fastest warrant response on record. Come on." He jerked his chin toward the door. "If you two are up for it, I'd like you along to tell me what I'm looking for and what I'm looking at."

"You couldn't keep us away," Parker said simply. He grabbed Mandy's coat from a rack beside the door and held it for her.

She accepted the small gesture, but couldn't help feeling as though she'd fallen into some sort of alternate reality where Parker actually acted like not only a normal guy, but a caring boyfriend.

As she preceded him through the door out into the hall, she couldn't help feeling that it was all a bit last mealish, which gave her the serious willies.

Trying to stifle the thought, she followed the men down the stairs and across the Atrium toward the main entrance. They were halfway across the open space, headed for the taxi queue outside the main admit desk, where Stankowski had double-parked his unmarked car, when someone called, "Mandy!"

She jolted and turned, and felt a different sort of discomfort when she recognized the figure hurrying toward them across the black-and-white checked tilework of the Atrium courtyard. "Kim! What are you doing here?"

The pretty brunette drew back, her normally cheerful expression clouding to confusion as she glanced from Mandy to Parker, and then to Stankowski. Her voice was cautious when she replied, "A woman delivered in Exam Three and I came down with the team to observe. I was on my way back up when I saw you." She paused, still looking at the men. "You swore to me you were okay. This doesn't look like you being okay. Are you in trouble or something?"

Mandy didn't answer right away, because how could she possibly answer? Tears threatened out of nowhere at the sight of her friend, and the knowledge that she might not be a Wannabe for much longer.

No, everything's not okay, she wanted to say. She wanted to lean on her friend, wanted to hug her, to cry all over her…but at the same time she didn't have the time—or the emotional energy—to go through it all right then. Not when searching UniVax Pharmaceuticals might give her the answers she needed.

She reached out and gripped Kim's forearm, needing the contact. "I'm sorry, but I *really* can't talk now. Can I call you later?"

Under other circumstances, Kim would've pushed for an answer, nagging her until she gave in. Maybe she sensed just how serious the situation was, or maybe she was intimidated by Radcliff's famed gruff temper, because she only shifted her touch, so her fingers linked with Mandy's, and squeezed reassuringly. "Sure, babe. Call me anytime."

Then she pulled Mandy in for an impulsive hug, before letting go and hurrying away. As she turned, Mandy thought she caught a glint of tears.

She glanced at Parker. "Any idea what the hospital rumor mill is saying?"

"I've tried to keep attention away from you being mugged the other day." His eyes were grave as he watched Kim disappear in the direction of the elevators that would take her back to the NICU. "Because of that, they're probably saying we're back together. No doubt there's a pool on how long it'll last this time, and whether you'll take off again when it's over."

Face heating, Mandy shot a look at Stankowski, who pretended sudden interest in the fountain at the center of the Atrium courtyard. He wandered a few feet away and dug in his pocket, ostensibly to flip a lucky coin in the water, in reality to give them a few seconds of semiprivacy to say what needed to be said.

But what was that, exactly? *Don't worry, if I manage to survive past the day after tomorrow, no hard feelings on the relationship front* didn't seem appropriate, and really it went without saying. She was using him for comfort and he was willing to be used. It was nothing more than that.

Rather, it *couldn't* be any more than that.

Which is why, instead of getting in any deeper than she already was, she lifted a shoulder and faked a shrug. "If you figure out who's running the pool, put twenty each on 'it'll last two days' and 'she'll stick around once it's over' for me, will you?" She smiled, and almost meant it. "I'm optimistic enough to think I'll be around long enough to collect."

She expected him to be relieved at being given a free pass on the conversation. Instead he looked at her long and hard, and there was something equally hard in his eyes when he said, "I'm going to damn well make sure you're around."

She knew he meant he was determined to

find a cure for whatever was inside her, but that didn't stop sly warmth from kindling.

To hide the response—and avoid thinking about what it might mean—she turned away and waved to the detective. "Let's go. We have an antidote to find."

THEY LEFT Boston General near 10:00 a.m. but it was early afternoon by the time Stankowski actually secured the warrant. The judge who had originally agreed to sign off on it wound up refusing to sign and then went incommunicado, forcing the detective to hunt down another judge. After a half-dozen wasted calls and trips, he finally managed to contact a notoriously difficult judge, who surprisingly agreed to sign off on the search.

While Stank went inside the courthouse to get the papers signed, Parker waited in an unmarked squad with Mandy, who'd been growing increasingly pale as the day continued. The rash had faded, but she'd battled a brief spurt of nausea, which only seemed to confirm that she'd been injected with the same cocktail as Irene Dulbecco.

It also indicated that, based on the other cases, they had less than twenty-four hours before she started showing pain symptoms.

Parker looked over at her. She'd leaned her head back against the back of the rear bench seat, and had her eyes closed. The pale cast to her skin made her look fragile and vulnerable, though the set of her jaw was anything but. The determination that was etched on her face, even when she was semi-relaxed, all but shouted that she intended to fight her fate to the last possible second.

Parker's chest tightened with frustration. He wanted to fix her, comfort her, to do something, anything to stop what was happening inside her. The delay chafed. They should've been inside UniVax Pharmaceuticals hours ago.

"What do you think happened with the warrant?" she asked without opening her eyes.

"Damned if I know." He blew out a breath and stared at the front door of the courthouse, willing Stank to appear. "It doesn't make any sense. Stank's been getting pressure from above to get the case solved so the local bigwigs living in the Patriot District feel safe.

But if that's the case, then why the sudden roadblock?"

"Maybe UniVax has powerful friends, too." Mandy opened her eyes and turned toward him.

Still lying back in the seat, she created an intimate picture that reminded him all too strongly of the night before, when she'd laid on his bed, waiting for him. Wanting him. Accepting him without reservation.

That's only because she's a little low on choices right now, Parker reminded himself. Under any other circumstances, he knew, they'd be locked in the same spiral as before, with her wanting more and him wanting out.

"Powerful friends," Parker repeated, forcing himself to focus on the conversation. "That's a possibility. Or…" He trailed off, not able to come up with a better suggestion. Shaking his head, he said, "Nope, that's probably it. That doesn't necessarily mean UniVax is dirty, though. Just that they have good lobbyists."

Moments later, the courthouse door swung open and Stankowski jogged down the steps.

"You got it?" Parker asked the moment the detective was in the driver's seat.

Stankowksi patted his pocket. "Signed and sealed."

Mandy leaned forward. "Did the judge tell you who was trying to block the warrant?"

"She wouldn't say, and I didn't press. I figured getting into UniVax is priority numero uno. After we've got you all cured and our mad scientist is locked up, then I'll do some sniffing around and figure out who's pulling the political ropes."

The detective pulled out onto Court Street and accelerated into traffic. The inertia pressed Mandy back against Parker, forcing her to brace a hand against his thigh.

When she leaned away, he covered her hand with his own and squeezed until she relaxed, leaving them sitting side by side, holding hands.

A short drive brought them to the building that housed UniVax Pharmaceuticals. Taking up most of a city block, the huge building housed offices and labs on one side, a warehouse and distribution facility on the other.

"Seems strange they didn't move their manufacturing and shipping out of the city," Mandy commented as Stankowski flashed his badge at a guard shack and was granted access to a small parking area that was clearly reserved for VIP guests and upper management.

"They've worked out some seriously beneficial tax breaks," Parker said, having called in a few favors for inside information on the company while they'd waited for the warrant. "They were talking about moving the entire operation to New Hampshire at one point, and even had the plans drawn up and contingencies signed on the land. Then the mayor stepped in—or some of his cronies did, I'm not entirely clear on who did what yet—and made them a deal they couldn't refuse, one that made it profitable to keep all their operations downtown, even with Boston traffic."

Stankowski parked and killed the engine. As they emerged from the car, Mandy stood and looked across the car roof at Parker. "Has anyone else noticed that this keeps circling back to politics?"

Stankowski's laugh was utterly without mirth. "You're in my business long enough, you figure out that eventually everything goes back to politics, especially in this city."

He grimaced as the trio crossed the parking garage toward a pair of glass-fronted doors marked with the UniVax logo of a DNA molecule twined around the earth. "But, yeah. I catch your drift. I'll put someone on figuring out who the pressure is coming from, and why. My best guess is that most of the politicking has nothing to do with the case, at least not specifically. On one hand, someone noticed a rash of crime near Patriot and used it to rile up a few powerful locals. On the other hand you've got whoever is profiting from UniVax, either politically or monetarily, or both. That side isn't trying to protect the killer or slow us down by blocking the warrant—at least not directly—but the net effect is the same. Delay."

"Too bad for them, I'm not in the mood for any more delays," Mandy announced, spots of color riding high on her pale cheeks. She pushed open the doors and marched through, with Parker and Stankowski at her heels.

They found themselves in a wide lobby that was done up as a museum of sorts, with digitized murals on the walls showing a timeline of scientific progress throughout the ages, with images shifting every fifteen seconds or so in a repeating sequence that represented everything from early experiments proving the existence of microorganisms to Watson and Crick's discovery of the double helix and later advances in human genomics and genetic engineering.

The ceiling was high above, and supported a half-dozen colorful mobiles shaped as different versions of six-carbon sugar rings, twisting in unseen air currents. At the floor level, the center of the open space was devoted to a bank of computer screens that invited the user to touch a series of icons and learn about UniVax's revolutionary product lines. Nearby, racks offered colorful glossy brochures, along with freebie key chains and imprinted pencils.

Parker found the whole effect dizzying with its profusion of color and movement, and faintly tacky with its emphasis on marketing. Then a different sort of movement caught his attention, and he looked beyond the computer banks in time to see a pair of elevator doors slide open.

A tall woman emerged, flanked by two

men who were dressed in high-end street clothes, but whose bearing and demeanor all but screamed "security."

The fortyish woman crossed the lobby, her two-inch heels clicking on the polished floor. Her dark hair was swept up into a twist and her sharp features were subtly and expertly made up. Her power suit was a deep plum color, and her jewelry consisted of yellow gold at her throat and discreet knots at her ears.

The whole effect was one of power and control.

Stankowski offered his badge. "Detective Stankowski. I'm investigating a series of murders that have recently been linked to a nanoparticle being produced by this organization. I'm going to need the names and contact information of everyone here who might have had access over the past two months."

She took the badge and glanced at it for show, but Parker sensed that he was the focus of her attention. His suspicions were confirmed when she returned Stankowski's badge, walked right past the detective and extended her hand. "Arabella Cuthbert, CEO of UniVax Pharmaceuticals. You're Radcliff, aren't you? I saw you speak last fall at the Boston Scientist's dinner. Fascinating stuff." Her handshake was firm, her expression dismissive. "I'm sorry to meet you under such... odd circumstances, though. Are you consulting with the police on this matter?"

Aware of Mandy bristling at his side, and time ticking away, Parker nodded. "That's correct. And before you ask, yes, the detective has a warrant. We need those names, and we need them ten minutes ago." He paused a beat, watching her eyes. "I would greatly appreciate your help here."

It was a tacit promise. *Work with us here and I'll swing some BoGen money your way.* It wasn't a game he liked to play, but it wouldn't hurt in the long run, and it might help them over the shorter term.

Unless, of course, they discovered that UniVax was somehow involved in the deaths and the danger to Mandy. If that was the case, he'd personally see that UniVax Pharmaceuticals in general—and Arabella Cuthbert in particular—went down in flames.

As if the promise of a favor owed to BoGen's head of emergency medicine was what she'd come downstairs looking for—no doubt warned by whomever had slowed the warrant process—she nodded and turned away. "Follow me. I have the files organized for you already."

Which cemented it—she'd been warned, damn it.

Parker felt the frustration—and the lost time—vibrate through him, tightening his muscles and humming through his bloodstream like rage, like loss. That anger redirected itself ten minutes later, though, when he found himself leaning over a computer terminal staring at a name that Arabella Cuthbert's data crunchers had starred for her, indicating that the employee had not only had access to the delivery system and the Dynastin 402, but he'd had disciplinary problems on the job.

More importantly, he'd been involved in the clinical trial arm of validating the delivery system, and he'd been fired three months earlier for letting trials go on long beyond when the toxicities meant they should be shut down.

And his file photo showed an angry-looking man with familiar, pale gray eyes.

"Dr. Paul Durst." Stankowski tapped the name on-screen. "Where can we find him?"

Arabella handed Parker a thin file. "Here are his employment records and other bits of information I thought might be helpful."

He scowled as he accepted it. "You were going to hand this over the whole time."

She dimpled, though the expression maintained a reptilian coldness. "Of course. But once I learned you were involved, I figured I could get a little something out of the exchange. Rumor has it you've got some big money coming in soon in the next grant cycle."

"Then you know something I don't," Parker said. He smiled at her, but expected that his expression was equally as cool as hers. "And don't think you're seeing any of it after this stunt. You could've given us this name six hours ago."

She lifted a shoulder. "Just business, Radcliff."

He bared his teeth. "Not to me, it isn't."

And just like that, he realized, all hope of detachment was lost. He was in way over his head, and sinking fast.

Unwilling—or unable—to deal with the

thought, he spun and headed for the door, shoving the file at Stankowski. "Come on. Let's find Durst."

Mandy stayed put, her eyes locked on Cutthroat Cuthbert. "Is there a way to reverse the delivery system, an antidote you've developed to block its effects and unbind the targeting sequence from its receptors?"

The other woman hesitated for a fraction of a second before she shook her head. "I'm sorry, but no. There would be no benefit in such a thing, because the delivery system should only be carrying beneficial molecules. Why would we want to reverse the effects?"

Mandy stared at her for a long minute before she said, "Why indeed?"

"How about a drug that causes nausea, followed by systemic pain?" Parker said, watching her reaction closely.

"Definitely not!" she said vehemently. "What do you think we are, monsters?"

"You wouldn't develop something like that on purpose, obviously." Parker looked pointedly at the handful of brochures he'd picked up in the lobby. "But I was thinking that maybe there was a painkiller candidate that wound up causing pain rather than blocking it…"

"No," she said firmly, dismissal clear in her voice. "Was there anything else?"

But as they were headed out of the building, Stankowski murmured, "She knows something."

"You bet she does," Parker agreed, anger crystallizing in his gut. "I hope you made friends with that last judge, because if we don't get what we need out of Durst, you're going to need an arrest warrant with her name on it."

"Count on it," Stankowski said, not even bothering to remind Parker that he was the cop in this equation.

As they climbed into the unmarked car, Parker felt something he hadn't felt in what seemed like a long, long time: hope tempered with fear. Hope that they might be on the right track, fear that they wouldn't be in time.

And both of them were emotions he could ill afford.

Chapter Ten

Mandy couldn't quell the nervous jitters as Stankowski drove them to the address on file for Paul Durst. On one hand she envisioned that they'd reach a dead end, finding that the address belonged to an abandoned lot or a Chinese restaurant, or that Durst had moved out weeks ago, after he lost his job.

On the other hand, though, she couldn't help imagining the relief of finding him, IDing him as the hooded man and discovering the raw materials he'd used to make his poison, along with a convenient store of the antidote.

"Hey," Parker said gently from beside her. "Try not to think about it. Stressing about it isn't going to change anything."

"You're right." She exhaled and forced

herself to relax into her seat. "I know you're right. Doesn't make it any easier to stay chilled out, though." She paused, and forcibly turned her attention to the folder he had open in his lap. "Anything useful?"

Instead of answering immediately, he looked at her for a long moment, then smiled faintly. "Atta girl." He took her hand and absently rubbed his thumb across her knuckles in a gesture he'd just developed starting that morning, one that tugged at her even though she knew it was the sort of thing he never would've done if he'd thought there was a threat of a future for them.

Reading from Durst's employee file, he said, "Not to bend the theory to fit the results or anything, but my gut says this all fits with what we've seen. Durst has a Ph.D. in biochemistry and coauthored a dozen or so papers on the early generation nanoparticles. He was at a mid-level university, which doesn't make much sense given his scientific production, unless we figure such a small place might not have had a strong ethics committee, meaning he could bend the rules more than he might've done elsewhere. About four years ago, UniVax wooed him away from the college and set him up here, giving him a pretty much unlimited budget as long as he delivered a functional targeting system within five years."

Knowing she'd get seriously carsick if she read over his shoulder, Mandy let her head fall back and stared at the interior of the car roof, thinking. "They fired him because his system failed its Phase II trials?"

"No. They fired him because he was hiding toxicities in the animal experiments, trying to push the targeting system through to human trials."

"Oh." Mandy didn't even bother trying to hide the shiver. "Then the muggings have all been some sort of perverse real-world beta test?"

"So it would seem." Parker closed the file as Stankowski double-parked in front of Durst's address.

Mandy was relieved to see that it wasn't an abandoned lot or a restaurant. Rather, it was an apartment building not unlike her own, generic and not in the best section of town.

"Not a very upscale address considering

what he's been making the past few years," Parker noted.

"Or he moved on long ago and his work records weren't updated," Mandy said, feeling her quick burst of optimism drain.

"We'll know in a minute. Backup's here." Stankowski popped his seat belt and climbed out of the car as two cruisers pulled up behind his vehicle. The officers who joined him on the sidewalk outside the apartment building weren't full SWAT, but they were wearing protective gear that drove home the reality that if Paul Durst was the hooded man, he was a murderer.

Feeling faintly nauseous, Mandy climbed out of the car and followed Parker across the sidewalk.

"Keep an eye on these two." Stankowski gestured for one of the officers to watch over Mandy and Parker. "Stay well back. I'll let you know when it's clear."

Parker looked like he wanted to protest, but didn't. Mandy figured they were lucky Stankowski hadn't dropped them off at the lab or ordered them to stay in the car. No doubt he would have, if it weren't for the seemingly slim chance that Durst would tell them something useful, or they'd see something in his place that would put them on the right track toward finding the antidote promised in the note.

Within the next few minutes, she might even be cured. It seemed so impossible she barely dared hope, but she was enough of an optimist that she hoped for exactly that. A cure. A future.

She glanced at Parker, taking in the square set to his jaw, and the flat, emotionless expression on his face. A few days ago, she might've seen only that outward facade, the cool disinterest he did his best to project to the world. She knew him better than that now; better, oddly, than she'd known him even back when they'd been lovers for several months in a row. The new knowledge allowed her to see the tension beneath the coolness, the caring beneath the lack of it.

It was possible that she was projecting again, seeing what she wanted to see, but she didn't think so.

This time it's real, she thought, and carried that certainty with her as she followed Parker into the building, under the watchful eye of their riot-geared protector.

Parker, however, was having none of being protected. "You do your thing," he told the officer in an undertone, pulling his gun from inside his jacket. "I've got this."

After a quick check with Stankowski, who reluctantly nodded, the young officer moved up to join the others, leaving Parker and Mandy to bring up the rear. The group moved into the stairwell, with one of the officers peeling off to put the elevators out of commission, blocking off escape in case Durst tried to run.

Stankowski gestured for Mandy and Parker to stay on the third level, waiting while the officers stormed Durst's apartment on the fourth floor.

When they were alone, waiting, straining to hear the sounds coming from above, Mandy whispered, "How well do you shoot?"

Parker surprised her by answering with more than a quick, "Well enough." Instead, he whispered, "My dad took off before I was born and my mother raised me alone. She was a cop with the Pittsburgh PD, and she took me to the shooting range when I was about thirteen and I started getting into the sort of trouble teenage boys get into. She taught me to handle a gun, and she ran me through the prison once, to give me an idea of where I'd end up if I messed up badly enough."

Mandy frowned, seriously confused. "I thought your family was from Long Island."

"The hospital rumor mill is like a vacuum—if you don't fill it up with something, it sucks up something else." He paused, attention focused on the doorway to the fourth floor. "Besides, the medical community tends to prefer dealing with their own kind."

It took Mandy a moment to digest that. "I get it. You're a reverse snob. That certainly explains why you always had a certain fascination with my family. You think that *I* think medical ability is genetically inherited."

"No, I think the entire community thinks that, but not because of genetics. Because of money, and the sort of education money can buy, as compared to scholarships, second jobs and Pell Grants coming out your ears." A muscle pulsed at the corner of his jaw. "But that wasn't what you asked. Back to the gun. My mother promised that if I kept my grades up and stayed out of trouble, she'd help me get certified for rifles, handguns and carrying concealed as soon as I was old enough." He paused, and his voice went hollow. "She was killed in the line three weeks before my eighteenth birthday."

"Oh," Mandy breathed, wincing with a sympathy she sensed he'd reject out of hand. "I'm sorry."

The knowledge explained a great deal, both why he was working in tandem with Stankowski and seemed almost more comfortable with police work than he did as a hospital big shot, and why he carried an instinctive dislike for people he perceived as being privileged, or maybe overprivileged. Including her.

She expected to feel the usual burn of resentment at being typecast by her father's reputation, but there was no anger, no nothing. It was as if the knowledge of her own impending death had helped her, if not forgive, at least move past what her father had done.

For the moment, at least.

She reached out and touched Parker's

shoulder, which was tense beneath her finger-tips. "I think—"

"Quiet." He held up a hand, and in the ensuing silence she heard running footsteps coming from one floor up. "Behind me," he ordered, moving so his body was between her and the door, and the gun was angled upward.

Mandy braced herself to see the hooded man as the door swung open. Instead, it was one of the riot-geared officers. He looked un-naturally pale beneath his gear, and swal-lowed hard before he said. "Stankowski wants you two. He's got something he thinks you should see."

THE DETECTIVE met them at the door to Paul Durst's fourth floor apartment, looking as grave as Mandy had seen him during their relatively short association. He gave them sterile gloves and booties to pull on, reducing the risk of crime scene contamination, and then waved them in. "This way, and make it quick. Once the others arrive, they're not going to want civilians on their scene."

Which meant that whatever they wanted to

show them had to be important, Parker knew. Stank might seem casual, but he was a by-the-book cop.

He led them through a good-size sitting area containing little more than the basics: a stiff-looking sofa and chair upholstered in neutral beige sitting on either side of a low coffee table that was bare of any books or magazines. There was an entertainment center against the wall, its racks empty of CDs or DVDs, though there were players for both tucked beneath the midsize television.

Off to the left of the four-room apartment there was a small kitchen nook with a dorm-size refrigerator, microwave and electric range-top. A few dishes sat in the drainer, but the nook, like the sitting area, was almost sterile in its neatness.

"Cleaning crew come recently?" Parker asked.

"Nope." Stankowski paused and shook his head. "According to the building manager, Durst stopped having them clean the place a couple of months ago. At some point recently, he changed the locks, too. The manager just noticed last week, when he wanted to do a walk-through with his contractor and get an estimate on some upgrades. He said he left a few messages on Durst's machine, and was planning on having a locksmith out, but never got around to it." He gestured to the first of two rooms opening off the main room. "Bedroom's there, lab on the other side."

"Lab?" Parker frowned at a heavy-built door that clearly wasn't part of the apartment's original design. If anything, it looked like the door to a meat locker. "He built a lab *here?*"

Mandy was already ahead of him, hurrying toward the heavy door, which was blocked open with a bulletproof vest, no doubt to keep others from contaminating any prints on the handle. She stepped through—

And stopped dead just inside the threshold.

"Oh, God," she breathed. "Oh, no."

Parker moved up beside her and his heart shuddered in his chest at the sight of a pretty blonde in her late twenties, maybe early thirties. Her features were eerily similar to Mandy's with one exception.

This blonde was very definitely dead.

Parker cursed, his words coming out on a puff of white courtesy of an open window that let in the winter air. The chill was augmented by a freestanding cooling unit in the corner. It hummed softly and emitted a faint mist, which rose past the white-painted walls to collect up against the laminate-coated ceiling. Condensation clung to every surface, forming beads of moisture on the chrome of a self-contained sink unit and a series of microscopes and centrifuges.

There was a high-lux fluorescent lamp set into the ceiling, and its cone of light shone down on a stainless steel table set in the dead center of the room…and the blonde who lay on it.

Her hair was fanned out away from her head in an artful halo, and her face looked almost peaceful in repose. A Y-incision had been carved into her torso and then stitched back up again, and tissue samples had been taken from her hands and feet.

"He autopsied her," Mandy breathed. "He injected her, tagged her and then used the transmitter to pick her back up later. Then he cut her open so he could figure out where his system was going wrong." She turned to Parker, looking seriously ill, like she was going to lose it. "The sick bastard's still doing his research, isn't he?"

"Not anymore," Stankowski said from the doorway. When they turned toward him, he jerked his head in the direction of the other room. "Durst is in the bedroom. He's dead, too."

Parker froze, then pinned the detective with a look. "Suicide?"

He got a slow headshake in reply. No other words were necessary: They'd gotten their guy, but he wasn't the end of the line. Someone else was involved—a partner maybe, or a boss. But who? Why?

"I'll stay here and look at—" Mandy began.

Parker cut her off, "No. You're coming with me."

The knee-jerk insistence was foolish, perhaps, but he didn't like the idea that there was more than one killer involved, and that he'd murdered his partner to prevent them from discovering…what? What was the next layer to this?

Mandy looked like she wanted to argue, but she acquiesced, following him away from the woman's body and out of the cold room.

As the crossed to the second bedroom, she said quietly, "She hasn't been dead long."

"I know," he acknowledged. The blonde's corpse hadn't begun to decompose significantly. Even given the cold temperature in the room, she couldn't have been dead for multiple weeks, which meant either it wasn't Missy Prieta—though it sure looked like her—or else she hadn't been injected right away. She'd been tagged during the mugging, then he'd taken her and kept her instead, using her as a human guinea pig.

On that grisly thought—and the burn of anger it brought with it—Parker paused at the threshold to Durst's bedroom.

The room was sparsely furnished with a bed, end table and small dresser. The bed was up against one wall, beneath a framed picture of flowers and children that had probably come with the furnished apartment. A pair of windows was no doubt intended to make the room feel open and bright, but now they let the cold winter light in to shine down on death.

Durst, a large man with short dark hair and an angry look on his face that persisted even into death, lay on the bed in the same position as the dead woman in the other room, flat on his back with his arms at his sides, palm-up, and his legs slightly apart.

Unlike the woman, though, he was clothed, wearing jeans and a plain navy sweatshirt that seemed jarringly normal after the scene in the other room. The pair of bullet holes in his temple, however, was anything but normal, at least in Parker's world. He shifted his body slightly as Mandy moved up beside him, trying to block her from the grim reality, but she pushed past him into the room, crossed to the bed and looked down at Durst.

"He can't tell us where the antidote is, and whoever killed him cleaned this place out," she said, her voice hollow. "It's a dead end."

"Maybe," Parker said, though in his gut he feared she was right. He crossed to her, careful not to touch anything more than necessary, and pressed his cheek to hers so their gloves stayed relatively sterile. "I'm not giving up, though."

"None of us are," Stankowski said, moving to join them. "We'll—"

A terrible explosion cut him off, roaring to life and flinging Parker into the nearest wall.

The bed was suddenly ablaze, the rug, the walls, the corpse—everything.

"Mandy!" he shouted as he struggled to his feet, his voice hoarse with the need to get to her, get her out of there.

"Parker!"

He turned and saw her staggering toward him, her hands outstretched, her body wreathed in flames. He grabbed her wrist and pulled her toward the door as Stankowski gained his feet and shouted, "Incendiary grenade, everyone out! There's going to be another—"

A second explosion obliterated his shout.

Chapter Eleven

Mandy screamed, but her voice was lost in the whoop of the alarm system and the roar of the fire, which was suddenly all around her. The heat, the terrible, awful heat made her skin feel crisp and her clothes burn where they touched her. She coughed, her lungs seizing on the smoke. Her mind cleared fractionally, and she realized she was pressed flat with something heavy on top of her. Trapped!

"Help!" she screamed, beginning to struggle. *"Help me!"*

"Quiet," a voice ordered from right beside her ear. "I've got you."

Parker, she thought, only then realizing that he was the heavy weight atop her. He'd used his own body to shield her from the second blast.

There was no time for gratitude, though. The fire was too hot, the smoke too thick. Squinting through the thick air, she could see flames, but she couldn't make out the door or windows, couldn't see anyone else.

"Where's Stankowski?" she asked, coughing the words like a longtime smoker.

Parker rolled off her, grabbing her arm and pressing down to keep her flat on the floor, which was growing warmer by the second. "Stank'll take care of himself. Let's get you out of here."

She didn't need to see his eyes to know it cost him to leave without looking for his friend. That knowledge was enough to keep her from arguing. "Lead on."

"Stay low, keep moving and don't look back, no matter what," he ordered, then levered her up and pushed her ahead of him in a hunched-over run. "Go!"

Somewhere up ahead she heard the rushing sound of water, then shouts. Moments later, there was a heavy thump and water rained down around them as the sprinklers cut in. The small streams did little against the inferno that was quickly engulfing the apartment.

Coughing, Mandy stumbled forward, tripping on something and nearly going down. The only thing that saved her was Parker's iron grip on her arm and the momentum of his big body pushing her along. Staggering and sliding on the increasingly wet carpet, she made it over what proved to be a piece of the coffee table.

"We're in the sitting room," she yelled, squinting against the smoke and flames and feeling as though her hair was on fire, her skin, her clothes, everything. "Where's the door?"

"That way!" He shoved her along a tangent and she complied, only to trip and nearly fall again.

This time, she'd stumbled over a person.

"Go!" Parker shoved her toward a patch of lighter air up ahead. "That's the door. And for God's sake don't look back, just *run!*"

Mandy did as she was told, ducking and running for the lighter air and finding the door with her outstretched fingers. Then suddenly there were others there, helping her. A uniformed officer grabbed her and hustled her out into the hall.

Despite Parker's orders, she looked back.

He wasn't behind her.

She saw Stankowski nearby in the hallway. His shirt was torn and his face was smudged dark with soot and smeared with a track of blood. She grabbed his sleeve. "Parker's behind me with one of the officers. He's—"

Before she could finish, a figure emerged from the smoke that billowed through the open doorway. Two figures, rather: a civilian dragging an injured cop with him.

Relief flooded Mandy, nearly painful in its intensity.

Parker was coughing, his clothes soggy, ragged and smoldering, and he favored his right arm when he passed off the cop. But he was alive. He was whole.

Not stopping for a second to think, Mandy flung herself into his arms on a sob.

"*Mandy,*" he said, and caught her against him, squeezing hard, squeezing the breath out of her as though he'd been afraid, as she had been, that they might never touch each other again.

She couldn't have said why that was suddenly so vital, why his safety was paramount now when he'd been her nemesis only days earlier. She only knew things were different now.

They clung to each other hard for a brief second, long enough to reaffirm that they were both alive, then broke apart as the cops hustled them down the stairs, away from the fire. In the stairwell, they joined a stream of frightened people being evacuated from the building.

They emerged from the stairwell, out into the small lobby, and from there to the street. The scene was utter chaos.

Three fire engines were already parked near the closest hydrants, and the wail of distant sirens indicated that others were incoming. People had gathered in loose knots of onlookers and evacuees, standing on the sidewalk or in the street, getting in the way even as additional officers and firefighters attempted to push them away from the burning building.

Mandy stumbled to a halt, turned and looked back. Four stories up, dirty smoke and flames belched from the window of what had once been Durst's apartment in a scene that was reminiscent of the smoke bombs in the M.E.'s office, but so much more than that.

A ladder truck-mounted hose had almost

reached the necessary height, and two firefighters were training the streaming water at the windows. On the ground, other firefighters wrestled with thick hoses, aiming gouts of water at Durst's windows, as well as nearby buildings and trees.

"It looks like they'll have it under control pretty soon," Parker said, his voice gravelly with smoke. "Doesn't do us much good, though."

"No," Mandy said faintly, almost too overwrought to be shocked anymore. "The apartment is gone, along with the bodies." She paused. "You know, there weren't any explosions until the three of us—you, me and Stankowski—were in Durst's bedroom together."

"I noticed." His voice was deadly flat, and he looked at the nearby buildings. "He must've planned it that way. Durst's partner—or his boss, or whatever—was watching. He wanted all three of us dead and the other two bodies destroyed." He paused, and the disgust was evident in his voice when he said, "Lucky for us, he didn't manage the first part. Unfortunately the evidence is toast, which leaves us nowhere."

"Not exactly." Feeling a mixture of shame and pride at her thoroughly illegal action, Mandy reached into the pocket of her jeans and withdrew a crumpled and torn piece of paper. "I—ah—sort of took a souvenir from the autopsy room. It was stuck beneath the confocal microscope."

When she opened the paper and smoothed it out, it proved to be part of a page torn from a laboratory notebook, showing part of a molecule schematic.

When Parker just stared at her, she shifted on her feet and said in a rush, "I know it wasn't right, but I figured whoever took all the other stuff out of the apartment must've missed this, or dropped it. Then I got to thinking that once the crime scene techs got it, it would take time for us to get copies. Maybe too much time. So I just..." She shrugged and looked down at the toes of her sneakers, which were soggy and nearly black with soot. "You know. Completely and totally broke the law."

She looked up, and saw that he was grinning.

He whooped, grabbed her around the waist and lifted her up, spinning her in an exuberant, completely un-Parkerlike display of excitement. Then he let her down again, and kissed her soundly on the mouth. "Nice job, klepto."

Then, quicker than she could keep up, he pushed her behind his body and snarled, "Hide it."

She crumpled the page and jammed it in her pocket just as Stankowski limped over to them. His dirty, battered face wore a thoroughly confused look. "What's up with you two?"

"Nothing," Parker lied. He locked eyes with the detective. "We need to get back to the hospital. I'll call you when I can."

Something passed between the two men, a silent moment of trust requested and received. Stankowski looked beyond Parker to Mandy, and it was clear the detective knew they were hiding something important.

Mandy held her breath.

Finally Stankowski nodded. "Okay. Keep me in the loop when you can. I'll do the same. My team is still working on the minidisk. It's either ruined or encrypted— they're making progress, but it's slow. In addition, after this blast the case will probably be kicked up higher on the food chain. That could mean some delays, whether we like it or not."

Translation: *You're on your own for the next few hours. Make the best of them.*

"Thank you," she said softly. "For everything."

He nodded. "See you soon. And good luck."

Tears pressed as she turned away and, with Parker sticking to her like a shadow, made her way through the gathering crowd toward the next block over, where they caught a cab and headed first to Parker's place for a quick shower and change—lest they get too many questions at BoGen—and then to the hospital.

There, hopefully, they would be able to decipher the schematic and find the antidote before it was too late.

FOUR HOURS AFTER they reached their commandeered lab space at BoGen, Parker and Mandy were still working on identifying the molecule shown on the stolen schematic. They were close to an answer, though. He could feel it in the tingle just beneath his skin and the pressure in the back of his brain, which were the feelings he typically got just before a patient's stubborn symptoms lined up into a diagnosis.

Or in this case, an answer.

"If it weren't for the substituted amino acids, we'd have it by now," Mandy said pensively. She sat back in her computer chair, stretching her arms out behind her and rolling her neck to work out the kinks brought on by four hours of nonstop database searches.

The schematic had proved to be a polypeptide that could be linked to the UniVax targeting sequence and the Dynastin 402 molecule.

Together, the three made up the full drug delivery system: the targeting sequence sent the drug to the proper organ system, the Dynastin protected it from diffusing before it reached its target, and the drug was some sort of miniprotein that caused pain and death.

Unfortunately, knowing all that still wasn't enough. In the absence of a way to flush the drug off the target receptor, they needed to figure out how to block the polypeptide itself, and they couldn't do that until they knew exactly what it was.

"It's not in the major databases, or in the

UniVax list Arabella Cuthbert gave us." Mandy scowled at the screen.

"It's got to be somewhere," Parker said under his breath. "Have you tried—"

"I've tried them all," she interrupted, voice sharp. "It isn't there." Then she stopped herself, and blew out a breath. "Sorry."

"Don't be. But don't give up on me, either. We're going to find this thing and we're going to fight it."

The pressure that had been sitting on Parker's chest all afternoon increased at the sight of her pale, lovely face set in resolute lines as she nodded and entered another query into the online database search engine maintained by the National Center for Biotechnology.

The NCB databases were comprehensive and contained almost every published gene or protein, save for those protected under the various national and international patent laws. All that information collected together in one place was the upside. The downside was the GIGO factor—garbage in, garbage out. If the researchers inputting the information messed up when transcribing a sequence, it might not show up on the search, or it might yield such a low match probability that the internal search parameters would automatically kick it out as a nonmatch.

Add that to the inevitable glitches that occurred in any search program handling a database of this size, and Mandy and Parker both knew that "no match" didn't always mean there wasn't a match, just that the search engine couldn't find it for some reason.

Unfortunately they *had* to find it.

As if sensing the weight of his stare, Mandy glanced over at him. "What?" She lifted a hand to touch her hair, which had dried quickly from her shower and was only a little frizzled at the ends from the heat of the fire at Durst's apartment.

That wholly natural, essentially female gesture sent a knot of something hard and hot up into his throat. He wanted to go to her, wanted to comfort her. Hell, he wanted to kiss her and press her back against the desk, wanted to take her there, in the computer nook of a borrowed lab. He wanted to imprint the taste of her, the feel of her and the sound of her cries as he took her over the edge with him.

He wanted to hang on to her and never let go.

Instead he looked away and cleared his throat. "Nothing. Just zoned out there for a second. Sorry."

Cursing himself for being a coward, for being the bastard his ex had always claimed, he refocused on the computer screen, keyed in a new search.

And got a hit.

He sat staring at it for a long minute. Could it really be that simple?

"You got something?" she asked from across the room, alerted by his sudden stillness, or maybe he'd said something, he couldn't be sure. All he knew was that he had an answer.

"Substance P," he said, voice nearly shaking with a reaction that wasn't quite emotion, but was sure as hell a long way from detachment. "It's a substituted, synthetic analog of Substance P. It's never been reported before, so I'm just going on the similarities, but that's got to be what it is."

She was at his side in an instant, leaning against him, her hair brushing his cheek as she read the data series on the screen.

"How did I miss that?" she said, almost to herself. "How did we not see it?"

"Because I was looking for a drug or a toxin and you were focusing on herbs. And because nobody in their right mind would ever use Substance P as a poison," he said. "It's a neurotransmitter, for God's sake."

She leaned closer, reaching across him to minimize the search screen and pull up a brief rundown on Substance P. "It's a natural molecule involved in nausea and pain responses..." she read aloud, skimming the page. "Yeah, yeah, we know all that...genetically engineered mice lacking Substance P appear to be immune to pain...great, but how do we deal with an overdose of the stuff?"

"I don't know," he said. "But I have a feeling I know who does."

AN HOUR LATER, Arabella Cuthbert and her lawyer arrived at the Chinatown Police Station and were immediately escorted to an interview room.

Parker and Mandy were already seated at the interview table when the UniVax CEO and her lawyer, a tall, distinguished-looking bald man with a disarmingly open smile, came into the room and settled themselves.

Mandy tried to catch Cuthbert's eyes, tried to send a mute appeal on a woman-to-woman level, but the CEO was careful to avoid her gaze.

Stankowski was running the interview, having slipped it in under the radar of his superiors, who were in the process of taking over the case. He stood near the back of the room with his hands in his pockets, his posture casual but his expression fierce.

"My client wishes to express her deep dismay at what Dr. Sparks has gone through, but wishes to reiterate that UniVax Pharmaceuticals is in no way liable for what has happened to her. Company records show that Paul Durst didn't remove the targeting system from company property. He must have purchased the components elsewhere and assembled them based on his work at UniVax."

"We'll see about that," Parker said with a pointed look at Arabella. "The police lab should have no trouble comparing the samples we got from Durst's place with material from your company. If it's a match, you're liable for whatever happens to Dr. Sparks."

Arabella's lips thinned, but she left it for her well-prepped lawyer to say, "As Dr. Cuthbert already told you on the phone, Paul Durst's side project on manipulating Substance P and its antibody was never sanctioned by the company, and she put a stop to his experiments the moment she learned of them."

"And no doubt kept samples of all his reagents," Parker said, voice reasonable, as though he were inviting her to share on a scientist-to-scientist level. "Just in case they proved useful down the line."

The lawyer considered this for a moment. "If…and I'm not saying they are, but if such reagents were in the possession of UniVax Pharmaceuticals, it would have to be understood that they are untested and unapproved for human use on any level."

"But he *did* make an antidote," Mandy said, pressing a hand to her stomach beneath the table. She wasn't sure whether the nausea was from the effects of the drug or pure nerves at this point.

"It's not approved," the lawyer repeated.

"There could be terrible side effects… If, of course, such a reagent existed."

Stankowski moved then, crossing the room to drop a piece of paper in front of the lawyer. "You'll like this. It's a release and hold harmless agreement."

The lawyer took a long moment to study the document, then looked at Mandy, really looked at her this time, as though he was seeing a person, not just an obstacle or a threat to his client's welfare. "You'd sign this?"

When she nodded, he passed the document to Arabella.

Mandy smiled faintly, though her stomach churned as she said, "Look at it this way, Durst will really get his wish now. I'll officially be a human guinea pig."

Now Arabella did lock eyes with Mandy, but she still leaned over and whispered into her mouthpiece's ear rather than answering directly. He said, "Dr. Cuthbert wants an additional assurance that you—or your legal heirs—won't prosecute UniVax for this unfortunate circumstance."

"I won't prosecute civilly," Mandy said, pulling a sheet of paper out of the folder in front of her, and sliding it across the table. She and Parker had prepared for this, too, with the help of one of BoGen's best lawyers. "You'll have to fight any criminal charges arising from Paul Durst's actions yourself."

A quick look at Stankowski's set expression was enough to assure both Arabella and the lawyer that there was no deal to be had on that front. After a whispered consultation that lasted far too long in Mandy's opinion, Arabella nodded, accepted a pen from her lawyer and signed both documents. She then passed them back to Mandy, who signed on her lines and slid them to Parker, who witnessed both documents.

And the deal was done. Mandy gave up her right to sue UniVax, and gave them the right to treat her with a completely untried drug.

She blew out a long breath and thought about throwing up. "So. What next?"

The lawyer lifted the lid of his briefcase and withdrew a clear plastic tube that was capped at both ends.

Inside it rested a loaded syringe filled with a clear liquid.

Mandy shivered at the sight, and at the

parallel. One shot to kill, another to save? Terrifying.

Arabella spoke for the first time. "From what I could gather from Paul's confiscated notes, you should inject all of it at once. Intravenous is best, but intramuscular if you have to."

"And after that?" Mandy asked quietly.

"In theory, the Anti-P will bump the targeted Substance P from the neural receptors. Once they've bound together, the Anti-P will display an antigen that is going to trigger an immune response, and your white cells will move in and degrade the P-Anti-P complexes."

Mandy swallowed hard. "How will I know that it's working?"

For the first time there was a hint of compassion in the other woman's expression. "If it works, you'll wake up tomorrow morning pain-free. If it doesn't, you won't."

Just as simple as that. Mandy shuddered at the prospect, but what was her other option?

Parker reached across the table, took the tube and tucked it into his jacket, beside the gun. Then he stood and gestured for Mandy. "Come on, let's get out of here."

He took her hand as they left the interview room, and kept it when they reached the curb outside the PD and he waved for a cab. Once they were in the taxi, he turned to her. "It'd be best to do this at Boston General, where we'll have all the equipment needed if there are side effects."

But it wasn't an order. It was a question.

She shook her head and felt a strange sort of peace descend. "Not the hospital. Take me back to your place. We'll do it there."

Chapter Twelve

Of course Parker argued that they should be at the hospital. Mandy insisted, though, and eventually got her way. She took it as a sign that he was worried about her whether he wanted to admit it or not—there was no way The Boss would've let himself lose a debate otherwise.

Or maybe she was projecting, because heaven only knew that she was sick with nerves, a blend of excitement at the thought that the Anti-P might work, terror that it might not.

She wanted to lean on Parker, wanted to draw comfort from his solid strength, but held herself away because she couldn't afford to show the weakness just then, lest he use it as leverage to strong-arm her back to the hospital. And if she knew one thing for certain, it was that she didn't want to spend

what might be her last night on earth in
Boston General.

She wanted to spend it in Parker's bed.

When they reached his town house, he
helped her out of the cab. She didn't need the
assistance—her legs were steady enough to
carry her through the nerves—but she let him
help because she liked the way he kept her
hand as they walked up the steps together.
She tried not to think *if only,* but it was hard
not to appreciate the domesticity of him
opening the front door and keying off the
security, and them walking in together, like
a real couple. Like the couple they might've
been if things hadn't fallen apart years ago,
like they might've been if they'd had a real
chance this time around, like they might be
if the Anti-P worked and—

Don't think it, she told herself. *Don't
even go there.*

The only reason he'd let her in as far as he
had was that she hadn't given him a choice,
and because there was a built-in end date for
their fling. If it had been open-ended, she
knew damn well he never would've given in.

"Let me take your coat." He reached out,

his fingers brushing against her nape and seeming to linger there for a second, bringing a tingle of awareness alongside the nerves. Once he'd hung up both of their coats, he gestured to the kitchen, looking uncharacteristically uncertain. "You want to eat something first?"

She blew out a breath, pressing a hand to her stomach. "No thanks. I'm feeling sick enough as it is." She paused, then said, "Let's do it."

He looked at her for a long beat before he said, "You're absolutely sure?"

"Do you have a better suggestion?" When he shook his head, as she'd known he would, she stiffened her spine and nodded. "Then yes, I'm sure. Shoot me up, Doctor."

"Take this." He handed her his cell phone and gestured toward the back of the main floor. "The light is best in the kitchen. I'll get the BoGen crash kit and meet you in there."

They didn't need to discuss whether or not it would be necessary to have the kit on hand. For all they knew, the Anti-P would send her into cardiac arrest before it had a chance to attack the targeting vector.

Then again, maybe it wouldn't, or maybe

one of the drugs in the lunchbox-size kit would be enough to keep her going.

It was those *maybes* they were depending on.

While Parker got the kit—and, she suspected, took a moment to steady himself— Mandy crossed to the kitchen and hiked herself onto one of the stools, so she could stretch her arm out on the small table and offer him a decent shot at the vein at the crook of her elbow.

Then she looked down at his phone, considering the implicit suggestion. *Call the people who matter most,* he was telling her without saying the words aloud. *This may be the last chance you get.* And he was right, but what could she say? It would take ridiculously long to explain the situation, and to what end? So her friends or her father could worry, too? That wouldn't change the outcome, and it would make her feel worse, not better.

Then again, her mother's death had taught her how hard it was to be the one left behind. That knowledge, more than anything, had her flipping Parker's phone open and dialing.

Kim answered on the second ring, voice guarded. "Hello?"

"It's Mandy." She worked to keep her tone breezy. "I still haven't replaced my cell yet, so I'm borrowing Parker's." She used his first name deliberately, hoping to tweak her friend's gossip radar and keep her away from the other issues.

It didn't work. "What in the name of little green men is going on?" Kim demanded. "And don't tell me that wasn't a cop you were with earlier. I saw him flash his badge at a lab tech downstairs the other day. Is there something you're not telling me about that mugging the other day?"

"I can't explain right now. I'm sorry. I would if I could, believe me." Mandy pressed the phone close to her cheek at the realization that the next time she saw Kim, she could very well be in a hospital bed, writhing in pain because the Anti-P hadn't worked.

Assuming, of course, that the side effects hadn't killed her right off the bat.

Suddenly the whole injection thing didn't seem like such a great idea, Mandy thought, straightening on the stool and pulling her sleeve back down.

"Then why did you call?" Kim said softly,

her voice a mix of concern and irritation, with concern predominating.

"I just wanted to hear your voice," Mandy said, trying to keep the tears from her own voice. "I wanted to say that I love you, and how lucky I am to have a friend like you. Without you, the Wannabes would've drifted apart long ago, and we would've missed out on the chance to watch each other grow up into the people we'd always wanted to be."

There was a long pause before Kim said, "You're scaring me, Mandy. Is Radcliff there? I want to talk to him."

"I'll call you tomorrow," Mandy said, and clicked off.

She sat for a second, thinking that she probably shouldn't have called. She'd just frightened one of the people she cared about most. But in a strange way, she felt calmer, as though she'd needed to touch that base.

Which meant there was one more call to make.

Vaguely aware that Parker was sitting out in the other room, waiting for her, she dialed a number and held her breath. She let it out in a rush when the call dumped to voice mail and her father's voice came on the line, inviting her to leave a message.

"Daddy, it's...it's Mandy. I was thinking about you today, and I just wanted to say I'm sorry. I was so mad at you after Mom died and you pretty much checked out...it wasn't until I got older that I realized it wasn't about me. You were grieving, too, and I couldn't see it. I still think you could've done better, but I could've tried harder to understand. Maybe we could've figured out something together." She paused. Knowing that this could be it, she said softly, "So that's all I wanted to tell you. I'm sorry, I understand, and...I love you."

She hung up without saying goodbye, and when Parker strode into the kitchen, she swiped the beginnings of tears from her eyes and shot him a rueful grimace. "He wasn't home. Typical."

But whether or not the message reached her father in time, she'd needed to make the call and say the words.

"You ready?" Parker lifted the tube, expression wary.

Incredibly, she found a laugh as she closed his cell phone and pushed it across the table toward him. "Don't worry, I won't gush all over you, too, and declare my undying love. I got it out of my system." She grimaced. "And yeah, I'm ready." She pushed up her sleeve and laid her arm on the table, palm-up. "Hit me."

His touch was efficient and impersonal as he swabbed the crook of her arm with a sterile wipe and used a finger to plump the vein. The needle went in smoothly and he hit the vein on the first try, and he pulled back a few drops of dark, deoxygenated blood before he pushed the plunger and fed the Anti-P straight into her bloodstream.

His touch might have been professional, but his expression was anything but. She locked eyes with him, and saw her own fear mirrored in his face as he withdrew the needle and set the syringe aside, then pressed a piece of gauze against the injection site, and took her hands in his. "Anything?"

"A little chilly when it went in, but other than that, nothing." Mandy's grin felt lop-sided. "Is that a good sign or a bad one, do you think?"

"A good sign. Definitely a good sign." He squeezed her hands. "Now, I guess, we wait."

"Actually I was thinking— Oh God." Mandy clamped a hand across her mouth and bolted for the bathroom, where she was thoroughly, miserably sick.

And so it began.

THE NEXT TWO HOURS were sheer hell for Parker, and he didn't think it ranked very high on Mandy's list of ways to spend an evening.

She alternated between chills and nausea, with the occasional fever spike for variety. At first she tried to shoo him away, preferring to retch in private. But he refused to go, instead sticking by her, and setting her up on the couch with water, ice chips and a bucket within easy reach.

At about the two-hour-and-fifteen-minute mark, in the brief lucid shift between chills and fever, she looked over at him, where he sat on the end of the couch with her feet in his lap, reading a dog-eared paperback. Her smile wasn't quite as crooked as it had been before, which was a good sign, but it definitely wasn't totally back to normal. Her voice was husky but clear when she said, "So much for 'ship 'em in and move 'em out,' eh,

Radcliff? I bet this is the longest you've ever spent with a single patient." Her eyes dimmed, her expression growing faintly misty. "Thanks for not calling a wagon to come and take me off to BoGen."

He shrugged. "You said you wanted to be here."

"Sort of a last wish?"

"No way," he said flatly. "And don't even think it. You're having side effects, that's all." He would've known exactly what kind if he'd been able to move her to Boston General, it was true. He could've run a battery of tests to see how her organ systems were doing, and whether her body had mounted an immune response to the nanoparticles yet. But that would've meant a whole lot of explanations, and it would've meant giving over some of the control to others. And in the end, he wasn't sure it would've mattered one way or the other. He had the crash kit on hand, and it looked like the only thing they could do was ride it out.

Maybe it made him selfish, but he wanted to be here, alone with her. Tending her.

Her teeth started to chatter then as another

chill gripped her, followed by the dry-heaves that were about all her stomach could handle at that point. But then, instead of swinging back to fever, the cycle quit. The heaves subsided. Her temperature stayed normal.

After ten minutes, her eyes started to clear.

"Ugh." She sat up gingerly, moving slowly, as though afraid to believe the miserable illness had passed.

Parker put down his book and turned to her, watching warily for a new symptom. "Anything?"

She sat for a moment, assessing, then shook her head and smiled with relief. "Nothing. I feel fine. Well, I'm achy and I could use a shower, but otherwise I feel okay. Better than okay, even. Almost borderline good."

"Give it a minute to make sure before you hit the shower, okay?"

When she nodded, Parker stood and, needing to do something to burn off the excess energy that had suddenly gathered in the wake of relief, he collected the cups of half-melted ice chips, and the other supplies he'd kept on hand, just in case he'd needed them. He took the debris into the kitchen and dumped it in the trash.

Then he leaned his forehead against the stainless steel fridge and shut his eyes.

Never again, he thought. He'd never go through something like that again if it killed him. He'd hated every impotent moment of it, had hated not being able to control her symptoms, hated that he'd been unable to do anything but wait for the illness to run its course.

For the first time he'd understood what his mother had been thinking when she'd gone into a friend's house without backup, responding to a grisly domestic abuse call with shots fired. He'd understood how she'd let emotion overrule common sense, how caring had made her vulnerable. How it had killed her.

He didn't want that, had never wanted it. So how had it happened?

Out in the other room, he heard her call, "I'm headed up for a shower. If you don't see me in ten minutes, it might be worth taking a peek and making sure I'm on my feet."

"Will do," he called back, never lifting his forehead away from the cool metal of the fridge.

He felt wrung-out and exhausted. Dispirited. And this was quite likely only the beginning. God only knew what other side effects might manifest themselves over the next few hours as the Anti-P kicked the Substance P off its receptors and triggered a widespread immune response.

He refused to consider the other alternative—that the Anti-P wouldn't work at all—because the only thing it seemed like he *could* control just then were his thoughts, and he'd be damned if they'd come this far only to have her—

No, he reminded himself. *Don't think it.* Because if he thought it, then he'd have to think about his own response to the possibility of her being dead within the next day or so, and he wasn't ready for that.

Upstairs, he heard the master shower come to life with a rush of water and the whirr of exhaust fans. The master bath was directly above the kitchen, because he'd decided to save money with shared plumbing lines when he'd planned the renovations. Now, the setup allowed him to stand in the kitchen like an idiot, picturing Mandy as she undressed and stepped into the shower.

He wanted to go to her, wanted to be with her, not only for sex, but to hold her, to make her feel better and let her know she wasn't alone.

Then again, she wasn't alone, was she? He'd heard the phone calls, heard her tell her friend and her father that she loved them. The words had come as easily to her as the sentiment did. She'd tried to explain it four years earlier, how love wasn't something to be afraid of, something to consider a burden or a problem. It just was, like the air. Like the beat of his heart.

He hadn't gotten it then and wasn't sure he got it now. Yet still, he wanted to go to her.

"Be a man," he said aloud, forcing himself to straighten away from the fridge. "Make her some food and put her to bed. Alone."

Him making love to her—having sex, whatever—the night before had been defensible. She'd needed the comfort and human contact. But things were different now. Everything was different, because it looked like—please, God—she had a shot at making it through this thing with her life, and that complicated matters.

Last night had been about endings. If they made love again tonight, it would be an attempt at a beginning, and he couldn't promise that. He'd never wanted to lose himself in the emotion she needed from him.

"I'm a selfish bastard," he said aloud. Why else would he be yearning for something that would only hurt a woman he—yes, damn it—cared about?

Cursing under his breath, torn between what he wanted to do and what he damn well ought to do, he spun toward the refrigerator. Then, helpless to do otherwise, he walked right past it into the sitting room, headed for the stairs.

Mandy was waiting for him halfway up, wearing a fluffy towel and a smile of invitation.

WHEN MANDY had stalled on the stairs originally, she'd thought she'd needed to talk herself out of taking what she wanted. Now, she realized she'd been waiting for him to meet her halfway.

When he did, when he emerged from the kitchen with his eyes hot and his jaw set, looking as though he knew exactly what he wanted, her heart leaped in her chest.

He crossed the room, his gaze never leaving hers, and paused at the bottom of the stairs.

Mandy felt her blood pulse in her veins, felt it rise up to flush the skin of her cheeks and throat. She tried not to think of the drugs in her blood, tiny molecules fighting a sub-microscopic battle for her life. Instead she concentrated on the moment, only the moment, as she stretched out a hand to the man she wanted, the man she was just now realizing was it for her. He was the one.

He always had been.

His fingers touched hers, linked with hers, holding fast as if he never wanted to let go ever again. Then they were climbing the stairs together, hand in hand, and walking to his bedroom without another word exchanged, and it was perfect. Absolutely perfect.

She'd set the lighting before she'd gone to get him; the soft glow from the bathroom night-light glowed in the faint mist from the heat of the long, bone-melting shower she'd taken. The moist air carried the scent of his soap and shampoo, along with the lighter fragrance of her body spray, which was one of her few feminine indulgences she'd retrieved from her apartment. The scents mingled, creating something that was part of them both, bringing a wash of heat to her body and a sneaky slide of warmth to her heart.

"Mandy," he began, "I—"

"Don't." She silenced him with the touch of her finger against his mouth. "Don't worry about it." It wasn't that she knew exactly what he was going to say, it was more that she didn't want to know. Not now. Not tonight.

Instead of saying anything more, she lifted her fingers to the buttons of his shirt and began to undress him.

If the night before had been about what he could make her feel, tonight would be the reverse. It was her turn. Her time. And though she refused to consciously admit that it might be her last time, that the antidote might not be working and the humming sense of wellness inside her was nothing more than the beginning of the end, the knowledge was inside her, making everything more poignant.

She knew it might be the end when she rose up on her tiptoes to kiss him as she undid his shirt, and the same knowledge was in his eyes when he pulled away and framed her face in his hands. He looked down at her for a long moment, then looked away, inhaling as though preparing to speak.

But he didn't. He just pressed her face into the hollow of his throat. They stood there, holding each other, their hearts beating in tandem.

"Oh, Mandy," he finally said, and there was a wistful note in his voice that she'd never heard before. But when she pulled away and looked up at him, he simply shook his head, leaned down and touched his lips to hers, and his kiss conveyed everything she needed to know.

Yes, it said. *I'm here. I care. If you wake up tomorrow morning, we can give it another try.* Maybe it even said, *I love you, too.*

She gloried in the kiss, returning it even as she finished with his shirt and pushed it off over his shoulders, leaving it to snag on his cuffs where his hands gripped her hips with increasing intensity. He changed the angle of the kiss, delving deeper, and she opened to him, glorying in the taste and feel of him, the potent male flavor on her tongue and the strong hardness of his body beneath her fingertips as she went to work on his pants.

When he reached for her towel, where she'd folded it over between her breasts, she backed away, leading him toward the bed.

"Let me," she said, and waited until he was standing staring at her before she undid the towel and let it fall.

She was naked beneath, and aching for him. The illness of an hour before was gone. In its place was a hum of heat and sensation.

A small corner of her brain recorded the escalating sensations and wondered if perhaps blinding lust was a side effect of the antidote, whether the unblocking of her pain receptors had triggered a pleasure response in its wake. The larger part of her didn't care one way or the other, though. Or rather, it knew that the lust was no drug side effect. It was Parker. Only Parker.

Without another word or hesitation, he shucked out of his shirt and pants, then skimmed his boxers down over his hips and stepped out of them, leaving him bare to her as she was bare to him. They came together, not with the heat and flame of the night before, but with the surety of lovers who had come back to each other and had no doubts this time.

Because of that surety, and the love she was just beginning to acknowledge, Mandy took control of the kiss, nudging him toward the bed and following him down.

Better yet, he let her take that control.

Feeling a thrill of power, she rose above him, letting her hair brush against the side of his throat, where his pulse pounded, evidence of the rush of blood beneath his skin and the heavy beat of his heart. They locked eyes, and his slow smile was all the permission she needed.

She sent her lips on a long cruise down his body, tasting here, nipping there, while he fisted one hand in the bedclothes, the other in her hair. His strong fingers massaged her scalp as his body arched beneath her. She could feel the tension in him, and knew what it cost him to let her have the upper hand, even here, in his bedroom.

That a man who so needed to be in control would let her control him here…that was the ultimate statement, the final proof that he trusted her. Maybe even loved her, she thought, and the emotion of it, the feeling of it grew within her, tangling around her heart and squeezing until she almost couldn't breathe.

For half a second she *couldn't* breathe, and panic flared at the thought that it was the toxin or the antidote, that she'd miscalculated. Then her lungs unlocked and she could breathe again, and with that breathing came a simple, irrefutable fact.

She loved Parker.

Despite—or perhaps because of—his irascible temper and many failings, she loved him. She hadn't spent the past four years pining for him, but she *had* been waiting. Waiting for their lives to circle back around to each other, waiting for him to be ready for what they could have together.

She could've gone to Michigan, could've gone to half a dozen other E.R.s across the country, but she'd chosen Boston, on some level hoping it was time for them now.

And it was.

Knowing it, believing it, *loving* it, she returned to his mouth, kissing him as she reached for the nightstand and found a condom. As the kiss spun out, he slid his hands along her body, from where her knees pressed into the mattress on either side of his big body, up her thighs and buttocks to her waist.

Heat flared in the wake of his touch. Need. Deciding in favor of expediency over control, she pressed the condom into his hand and waited while he opened the packet and donned the latex barrier without breaking the kiss.

Then he tossed the empty wrapper aside, returned his hands to her waist and urged her downward.

Knowing she'd been ready for him since the moment she'd stepped out of the shower, she slid down onto him in a single strong move.

He filled her. Stretched her. Completed her. With his hard flesh seated to the hilt within her, she paused for a breathless instant, absorbing the sensations, reveling in the heat.

Then, with his hands on her hips and her lips against his, she began to move, building the rhythm slowly at first, and then faster and faster as the heat flared between them and her body demanded not gentleness anymore, but the slap of flesh against flesh and the groan of the man beneath her.

He met her thrust for thrust as she strained toward the first peak, hovering near but not quite reaching the pinnacle until he broke with a shout, wrapped his arms around her waist and neatly reversed their positions. With him above and her below, he thrust home, touching her deeper with each sure move. She cried out and arched against him, wanting more, demanding more, and he gave and gave and kept giving until she was there.

She cried his name as the pleasure spun out and then coalesced, and she was coming in glorious waves of release. Of a new beginning.

He groaned deep in his chest and followed her over, and the pulse of his flesh within her prolonged the orgasm, drawing it out until they collapsed against each other, spent with pleasure.

At some point they both fell asleep, still intertwined.

Later, when the moon had come and gone, they turned to each other again and made slow, soft love as morning approached and the hours counted down.

When the alarm went off at 6:00 a.m., Mandy woke with a jolt, her eyes flying open and her hands grabbing for the nearest solid object, which turned out to be Parker.

"I'm alive," she said, knowing it was stupid but needing to say it just the same. As a groggy Parker rolled over to face her, she ran a quick mental inventory and didn't find so much as a twinge of pain. "Nothing hurts!" She leaned in and kissed him hard on the mouth, then threw her arms up in victory, not caring that the sheet slid down and she was naked beneath. *"It worked!"*

When that didn't seem like a sufficient celebration, she jumped up and did a little dance around the room.

It was a cold morning; frost furred the sun-brightened windows and the air in the bedroom was sharp despite the town house's central heating. Mandy's skin tightened and her nipples hardened to buds, and she spun, thinking about diving back under the covers with Parker and putting her sudden burst of energy to good use.

Then she got a look at his face, and stopped dead.

Chapter Thirteen

"Oh, hell," Mandy said, her stomach plummeting to her toes at the absolute stillness of his body, and the closed-off blank of his expression.

He sat in the center of his bed, and though it was a king-size mattress, it suddenly seemed as though there was only room for one person. He looked, if possible, even more unreachable than he had the first time he'd seen her back at Boston General and hadn't even blinked.

Even worse, he looked trapped.

The cool air on her skin, which had been invigorating only moments before, was suddenly harsh and punishing. She crossed her hands ineffectively over her breasts and inwardly cursed herself, cursed him. Aloud, though, all she said was, "I'll go get dressed."

She escaped to the guest room, pulled on underwear, jeans, a shirt and socks at random, and jammed the rest of her things in the leather duffel she'd brought with her from her apartment. She knew the danger wouldn't truly be past until Stankowski and the others had caught Paul Durst's killer, which meant she couldn't go back to her apartment yet, but she'd be damned if she spend another night in Parker's town house. Not because of the way he'd just looked at her, or because of their inevitable parting, but because she'd gone and done it again.

She'd fallen for him when he didn't feel the same. Not even close.

"Mandy, I'm sorry. I wish I could promise to give you what you want," he said from the doorway.

"Don't bother, I get it." She zipped the duffel, then looked up at him. He stood in the doorway, looking as though he'd dressed as hurriedly as she. His hair was still bed-messy and he was wearing last night's jeans and the Harvard sweatshirt without another shirt underneath.

Only the day before, she would've imagined sliding her hands into the warmth beneath that sweatshirt, and touching the man beneath. Now, all she could think about was getting the hell out of there.

Running away again? her inner voice demanded. *You haven't grown up as much as you thought.*

The realization had her blowing out a long breath and pausing in her flight. She stood and faced him squarely before saying, "Look, I made the ground rules and I broke them by thinking we might have a chance at something more. That's on me. But if you don't think there's something special between us, something that could be wonderful if you let it, then you're an idiot."

For a second she imagined a hint of warmth in his eyes, and felt a burst of hope that he might give it a chance after all.

Then he looked away and shook his head. "I don't want what you want. I've been married, and it doesn't work for me."

"Because you won't let it. Because you won't let anyone inside." Defeat pressed on her chest, squeezing her heart until tears seemed like the only option. "But like I said, my bad for thinking you'd changed."

"Mandy…" He trailed off, because they both knew there was nothing else to say.

"I'm out of here." She shoved her feet into her sneakers, yanked the laces tight and stood, swinging the duffel over her shoulder. Holding up a hand to stem his protest, she said, "I know. I won't go back to the apartment, and I'll stay in plain sight. I'll even carry your cell if that'd make you feel better. But please don't ask me to stay here and be civilized—I'm just not feeling it right now. It wasn't your fault I got in too deep, but that doesn't mean I want to hang out with you, either."

She marched toward the door, expecting him to back off and take the easy way out, because he'd never been one for personal confrontations. When it came to professional arguments he was a pit bull, but on a personal level he'd always preferred to ignore the issues until they packed their bags and left.

Well, she was packed, and she was leaving.

He didn't budge from the doorway, though.

"Wait," he said quietly, as if him blocking the damn door wasn't enough to prevent her from going. There was a thread of unexpected sadness in his voice when he said, "I didn't mean to hurt you."

"My emotions, my problem." She dredged up a rueful smile. "Besides, I have a few things to thank you for, too. Like the fact that I'm alive. If it hadn't been for you, I don't think I would've made it through the past few days."

But at the same time, the danger had forced her to put a few things in better perspective. It was time to start living the life she wanted to live, and that didn't just include career goals.

She wanted a partner damn it, and a family. She was done wishing for something Parker couldn't give her.

So when he just stood there, looking as though he wanted to explain something to her that he couldn't even explain to himself, she shook her head. "Don't stress about it, boss. Let's just let things go back to the way they were. The hospital part of the investigation is over. I'll stay on my toes until Stankowski closes the case, and then we'll just…go back to normal, I guess."

He looked at her strangely. "You're not going to leave Boston General?"

A crooked smile touched her lips. "I'm a big girl. I can take disappointment without turning tail and running." She would do it, too, partly to get the fellowship and partly to prove to herself, once and for all, that she was over him. And if that thought brought an all-encompassing ache to the region of her heart, she was the only one who needed to know about it.

She stepped forward, forcing him to give way unless he was willing to physically bar her from leaving.

He retreated, but followed her down the stairs, making her feel as though he was escorting her to the door. "I'd feel better if you stayed here until Durst's killer is in custody."

"No, you wouldn't." She grabbed her jacket from the rack just inside the door. "I'll take a cab straight to Boston General. It'll be fine, really." She forced a smile. "I have some serious work to catch up on, and you know how my boss can be about productivity."

As she reached for the doorknob, she realized that part of her was waiting for him to stop her. *Stay here,* she wanted him to say. *Don't leave me.*

But of course he didn't say that. He never would.

Instead he said, "Give me five minutes. I'll call a cab and get dressed."

They rode in to Boston General together, sitting in strained silence. Just inside the E.R. doors, they paused awkwardly, already the targets of curious glances from the front desk staffers and a couple of paramedics on their way out for another ambulance run.

Mandy gestured toward the desk, and the staff lounge beyond. "I guess I'll go change, sign in and get started on the day."

"Yeah." Parker stuffed his hands in his pockets and scowled. He started to say something, but broke off with a curse, finally saying, "I'll let you know if Stank has anything to report."

Then he strode off without a backward glance, headed for his office.

Mandy stifled a sigh at the thought that they were going back to business as usual. She'd avoid him, he'd ignore her, and never the twain shall meet. Or something like that.

Frustration dogged her steps as she passed the front desk, even though she reminded herself she was supposed to be rejoicing. She was alive, damn it. She had time to figure out the rest of it.

"Dr. Sparks?" Aimee called as she passed. When Mandy turned back, the hugely pregnant staffer said, "There's a patient waiting for you in Exam Three. He said he was referred by a detective or something?" There was a definite question in the woman's voice, inviting an explanation.

Mandy ignored her and hurried to the lounge. "Let me change and I'll be right there."

She thought about calling Parker, but vetoed the thought. She needed the space and suspected he did, too. Besides, for all she knew, Stankowski had given out her name because she was the only one he knew in the E.R., save for Parker, who rarely saw patients anymore.

Once she'd shucked off her jacket and changed into scrubs and the white coat she kept all her ID badges and little accessories in, she headed for Exam Three, pushing open the door with the reassuring smile she used with all her patients. "Good morning, I'm Dr. Sparks. What can I—"

She broke off and stopped dead when she

saw that the narrow bed was empty, but she was too late to turn and run. The "patient," who had been standing behind the door when it opened, clamped a gloved hand across her mouth and banded a heavy arm across her torso just below her throat.

Panicked, Mandy screamed and thrashed, but the sound was muffled by the man's hand and her struggles were ineffective. He barely reacted at all, merely hauled her off her feet and held her just off the floor. Then he leaned his face close to hers and said into her ear, "We can do this the hard way or the easy way, Amanda. You pick it."

She bit down on his hand.

He cursed and shook her, then said, "Okay, the hard way it is."

Pain flared in her arm, followed by a numb fizz as she slid into the darkness.

PARKER LASTED thirty minutes in his office, pretending to do busywork, before he decided to call Stankowkski.

It was either that or head down to the E.R. and try to pick up where he and Mandy had left off that morning—and that was a recipe for disaster, because he wasn't even sure what he wanted to say to her anymore. He'd thought he'd known the right answer the night before, when he'd decided to let her sleep alone, but then she'd come down the stairs and crooked her finger at him, and he'd been lost, only to have reality return in the light of day.

She needed more than he could give. It was as simple as that, and as complicated.

So instead of picking another fight neither of them would win, he called Stank. "Any luck?" he said without preamble the moment the detective answered his cell phone.

"Yes and no. We don't have the partner's name yet, but we're getting closer. One of the guys on my team is into local politics, and he figured out that all of the muggings took place in the areas covered under a new crime prevention bill that's slated for review in the next few weeks."

Parker frowned. "You think someone planned the attacks to push the bill through? That's…"

"Creepy. I know."

"I was thinking more along the lines of

'not the dumbest idea I've ever heard,' but 'creepy' works, too." Ignoring the beep of another incoming call, Parker paused for a moment. "You have a handle on which politicos and companies are going to benefit most if the bill goes through? Any ties to UniVax?" He still couldn't get past the idea that Arabella Cuthbert was involved somehow.

"I've got a team headed over to UniVax now," Stank replied with grim satisfaction. "I don't have anything new, but it never hurts to rattle the trees and see what falls out. I have a feeling we're closing in on this thing. With any luck, it'll be wrapped up in the next day or so and you can get back to business as usual." He paused. "Or, as I should say after seeing you and Dr. Sparks together over the past few days, business not-quite-as-usual?"

"No, you were right the first time. I'll catch you later." Parker hung up with a shade more force than absolutely necessary, then told himself to chill. He was doing the right thing, damn it.

And if he told himself that a few hundred more times he might even believe it, he thought, rubbing his chest, where an ache had gathered in the vicinity of his heart.

Remembering the call that had beeped in while he'd been on the phone with Stank, he hit the playback button on his voice mail, and clicked it to speaker.

A buzz and a hiss sounded in his office, followed by a mechanized, mechanically altered voice. "There's a package for you at the front desk," the voice said. "Open it in private and don't tell anyone—especially your cop friends—about this call, or she's dead."

There was a pause, and Mandy's voice came on the line. "Parker? I'm sorry. I—"

The message cut off abruptly, leaving Parker sitting frozen in shock with his fingers hovering over the handset.

Then he exploded from his chair and bolted out the door toward the E.R. His heart drummed Mandy's name in his ears as he ran down the short hospital corridor and skidded around a corner, nearly wiping out an oncoming gurney-strapped patient and the medical team surrounding him. There was a flurry of activity and apologies and he was off again, pounding toward the front desk. He was aware of the curious looks he was getting, not because a doctor running was an unusual sight in the E.R., but because that doctor was The Boss.

He skidded to a halt at the front desk and snapped. "A man left something for me."

Aimee went wide-eyed and handed over a flat envelope. "Is everything okay, Dr. Radcliff?"

"No." He grabbed the envelope and lunged past the desk, into the lounge, which was thankfully deserted.

The moment he had the envelope open, the disposable phone inside began to ring. He looked around wildly, trying to figure out how the bastard knew he'd gotten it, where he was watching from, even as he flipped the thing open and snarled, "If you've hurt her—"

"Shut up and listen," a voice interrupted. It was a man's voice now, not the flat, mechanized version of before. "Your girlfriend is being smart, and she's decided to cooperate. If you're equally smart, you can have her back unharmed."

Parker's fingers dug into the cheap plastic

of the phone, making the unit creak in protest. "What do you want me to do?"

"She says the cop has the minidisk. You're going to get it back without telling him a damn thing. Once you have it, go back to your place alone. I'll contact you with further instructions." The man paused. "Do I need to spell out what will happen if you fail to follow instructions, or if you clue in your cop friends?"

"No," Parker gritted. "I get it."

"Good."

Sensing that the other man was about to cut the connection, Parker said, "Wait!"

At first he thought he'd been too late, but then the voice said, "What." It wasn't really a question.

"Let me talk to her, or there's no deal."

"You're not exactly in a position to be making demands." But there was a shuffle and a rustle on the other end of the line.

Then Mandy's voice, sounding shaky and tear-filled, said, "Parker? Don't—"

"Hush," he said quickly, his heart squeezing in his chest. "And hang on. I'll be there soon. I—"

The line went dead, leaving him standing

in the staff lounge with his free hand clenched into a fist. He wanted to hit something, wanted to rip the man on the other end of the phone to shreds with his bare hands. He felt the situation spinning away from him, out of control.

Someone else was calling the shots now, and he couldn't handle that. Problem was, he was going to have to deal, or risk Mandy's safety. To hell with forgetting about people the moment they were out the door; he'd been deluding himself if he ever for one moment thought that he'd forgotten about her. She'd been lodged inside him, waiting for him to grow up enough to admit it.

And if that meant that he was finally growing up, then so be it.

Under any other circumstance, with any other person, he would've gone to Stankowski and turned over the phone and his voice mail recording, and washed his hands of the situation. Since it was Mandy, he yanked off his white coat, grabbed his jacket and bolted for the main entrance, planning on following her captor's instructions to the letter, hoping against hope that he would play fair.

Problem was, the bastard had already killed one accomplice, which suggested he didn't plan to leave any witnesses behind.

Chapter Fourteen

"Watch him carefully," the navy-suited man snapped into a cheap cell phone. "If the cops mobilize once he's gone, call me on this line and we'll go to plan B."

Mandy closed her eyes and tried to wish the scene away. She was gagged and bound to a chair in one corner of a cheap-looking, one-room studio apartment. The shades were drawn, but daylight leaked around the edges and the lights were on, revealing a sofa bed upholstered in nubby brown fabric on one side of the room, with a small TV opposite it, next to her chair. A small table in the eat-in kitchen nook was missing one of its ladder-back chairs, no doubt because she was sitting in it. Two cases of diet soda and a few bags of chips on the kitchen counter were the only signs of habitation, suggesting that the men had rented the place just for this purpose.

For her *kidnapping*. Mandy still couldn't believe what had happened, what was still happening.

The three men, the slick guy in the suit and two rougher-looking thug-types in jeans and leather jackets, all three armed with handguns, had talked freely in front of her ever since she'd regained consciousness. That, and the fact that they hadn't bothered to disguise their faces, made her think that no matter what they told Parker, they weren't letting her out of there alive.

More importantly—and terrifyingly—she could ID at least one of them; she recognized Blue Suit from the evening news. He was one of the newcomers in the upcoming congressional race, Deighton or Leyton or something. Deighton, she thought, and wished she'd paid better attention to the news instead of channel surfing from one cop drama to another.

Watching him interact with his two underlings before he'd sent them to follow Parker and report his actions, Mandy had seen the coldness in the handsome politician's face. It was more than the chill control Parker often showed, though. No, Deighton's lack of warmth was far more unemotional, far more terrifying.

Parker, she had realized, tried very hard not to care. Deighton simply didn't care in the first place, and that was a big difference.

A potentially deadly one.

When he clicked the phone shut, he glanced at her, eyes hooded. "Your boyfriend better behave."

Gagged, she couldn't respond. Besides, what could she have said? They weren't boyfriend and girlfriend, weren't anything except the possibility of what might have been if he'd been different, if he'd cared for her enough to risk loving her.

At the thought, at the sure knowledge that she might never see him again, her eyes filled with tears. One spilled over and tracked down her cheek, then followed the line of duct tape plastered across her mouth.

She'd caught the gist of the situation from overhearing the men's conversation and could fill in the gaps with educated guesses. Paul Durst, it turned out, might've been a scientist who'd gone off the deep end but he wasn't stupid. He'd clandestinely taped his conversations with Deighton as a form of insurance. He'd also taped his attacks, no doubt as part of his "scientific data." The pocket unit had gotten banged around during his struggle with Irene Dulbecco, and the disk had come loose. Durst hadn't been able to find the disk in the alley; figuring it had been thrown out with the latest garbage pickup, he'd returned to business as usual, identifying Mandy as Irene Dulbecco's doctor and deciding she was just his type—blond and pretty, like Missy Prieta—making her perfect for his next trial run.

Deighton hadn't realized what was going on until one of his political contacts within the police department mentioned the minidisk.

He'd gotten lucky with the damage to the disk, but couldn't run the risk that the techs would pull anything useful off it, especially after Durst confessed that it had contained enough information about planted crime waves and dirty dealings to blow Deighton's campaign—and his career—out of the water.

Deighton had given the scientist a simple

choice: get the disk back or die. Paul Durst, however, was never one to miss an opportunity to advance his version of scientific progress. He decided to dose Mandy with the toxin and offer the antidote in exchange for the minidisk.

After that, Mandy was unclear on the details, but she could guess at them. Paul Durst had failed to transmit the ransom demand, most likely because he'd been unable to find the information he was looking for in his autopsy of Missy Prieta, and was planning on grabbing Mandy when she started showing symptoms. Deighton found out about the betrayal and killed Durst, and then when he realized Mandy had survived, came up with a last ditch plan to get his hands on the minidisk: kidnap and ransom, plain and simple.

Except in this case there was no promise of an antidote, only the lie that he would set her free if Parker brought the disk and didn't involve the police.

He wouldn't let her go, though. She knew too much. She'd seen his face.

At the knowledge, the tears broke free just

as the phone rang and Deighton answered with a sharp, "Talk to me." He listened for a moment, expressionless, then said, "Stay on him. If he so much as scratches his nose in a way you don't like, call me and I'll take care of the loose end and get out of here." He glanced over at Mandy, leaving no doubt that she was the loose end.

She shivered at the confirmation that there was very little chance of her getting out of the crummy apartment alive. But if that was the case, why keep her alive this long?

Because he wants Parker, too, she realized with chill certainty. Maybe he intended to use Parker to put pressure on Stankowski, or maybe he thought Parker's attachment to her was deeper than it really was, and feared that he'd seek retaliation for her death.

Not likely, she thought with a flash of bitter anger. *He'll just walk away. Out of sight, out of mind.*

He'd regret her death, no doubt, but it would no more change his life than her departure four years earlier had done, i.e. not at all.

For the first time, though, that realization didn't bring sadness or even anger. It brought her stubborn streak to the fore. He didn't think he needed her? Well, he was just plain wrong about that. He needed her to keep him from getting stuck in his own rut, needed her to brighten his world with more than a few spider plants, needed her to force him to give her a chance, to give *them* a chance.

None of which was going to happen if she just sat there, waiting for the moment he showed up with the minidisk and Deighton killed them both.

Done with passivity, she narrowed her eyes and looked around the room, trying to come up with a plan. As she did so, she tugged sharply at the nylon ropes securing her wrists behind her back.

The chair creaked, bringing Deighton's head up. Scowling, he stalked across the room, dragged her away from the wall, chair and all and checked her bindings. Satisfied, he muttered something under his breath and returned to the position he'd held before, standing just to the side of one of the windows, peering through the gap between the blinds and the frame, idly toying with his gun, sliding the safety off and then on again with rhythmic clicks. Off, then on. Off. On.

Mandy let out the breath she'd been holding, then shifted experimentally to see if what she thought had just happened actually had. When she moved her shoulders against the back of the chair, it creaked, more softly this time, and she felt one of the ladder-back slats give. She cupped her bound hands and moved again, and this time the slat fell free into her fingers, pricking her with the sharp end of a nail.

Forcing herself not to react outwardly and attract Deighton's attention, she fumbled to set the nail against her bindings, and got to work.

PARKER was no expert at the covert stuff, but he was pretty sure he was being followed as he reached the police station. When he opened the main entrance door, he glanced back in time to catch the two guys who'd been tag-teaming him pause warily on opposite sides of the street.

He had to assume they wanted him to know he was being followed, as another level of warning. More importantly, based on the tracking implants Durst had used on his victims, he had to assume he'd been bugged, and that either his pursuers or the man holding Mandy would be listening to—and possibly even watching—him as he tried to get his hands on the minidisk.

He had to assume the worst, because if he didn't assume they were listening and watching, then he'd be tempted to find some way to signal Stank. If the thugs caught the signal, though, it would mean the end for Mandy. He'd heard it in the other man's voice.

No more games.

"Can I help you?" the desk officer asked automatically before looking up from his log book. When he recognized Parker, his expression warmed. "Hey, Doc. Stankowski is out in the field. Can I help you?"

"He sent me to pick up something for him. Is it okay if I just go on back?"

The desk officer waved him past. "Just remember to sign it out under Stank's badge if it's evidence." They weren't supposed to allow such things, but Stankowski had okayed it before under extreme circumstances.

Little did the younger officer know, these were the most extreme of circumstances.

Sweating lightly, expecting to hear shouts and footsteps at any moment, Parker let himself into Stank's office and crossed to the desk. He popped a fake rock off its magnetized anchor on the underside of the desktop and shook out a small key, which he used to unlock the lower right-hand drawer, where the detective tended to keep checked-out evidence from ongoing cases. Parker held his breath, hoping Stank had held true to form with the evidence from this one.

Sure enough, the minidisk was neatly labeled and filed in the drawer as though waiting for him.

"Sorry, Stank," he said aloud, knowing that this one act would probably get him booted out of his consultant role at best, land his ass in jail at worst. Either way, he feared it could spell the end of his friendship with Stankowski.

He'd do it, though, for Mandy. He'd do anything for her...except, of course, tell her that he'd do anything for her.

"Which only proves that I'm an idiot." Remembering the likelihood of a bug, he shut up and moved to close the drawer. At the last second, he reached in, grabbed another evidence envelope and stuck it in an inner pocket of his heavy leather jacket, where a casual search might not find it.

Come on, Stank, he thought. *Be as smart as we both know you are.*

He didn't say it aloud, though. He didn't dare. Instead he stuck the minidisk in his pocket, relocked the desk and returned the key to its fake rock. Then he left the way he'd come in, sketching a wave at the desk officer and holding his breath in the hopes that Stank hadn't called in and blown his cover story.

The officer, who was busy on the phone, barely looked up as he returned the wave.

Then Parker was out on the sidewalk, and he could breathe again. Moments later, he was in the street, hailing a cab. "Beacon Hill," he said even before he got the taxi door shut, giving the address. "And step on it."

As the cab joined the streaming traffic, he glanced back to see the two men who'd been following him both climb into a parked car together, apparently either assuming he hadn't made them or not caring one way or the other. He figured on the latter, which should have intimidated him. He wasn't intimidated, though. He was furious.

More importantly, he thought as he settled back in the rear of the cab and felt the bulge of his gun press beside his spine, he was armed. Maybe this wasn't what his mother had envisioned when she'd brought him to the range all those years ago, but she'd led by example. She'd stood up for—and died for— what was right. For the people she'd loved.

Parker could do no less.

Chapter Fifteen

The landline phone in Parker's town house was ringing when he let himself through the door. The two guys who had followed him were nowhere in sight, making him think he was, indeed, bugged. He reset the security system behind him, thinking to slow the others down if they wanted to come in after him—or even better, alert the cops if they tripped the alarm. Then he crossed the sitting room and grabbed the phone on the sixth ring, right before it dumped to voice mail.

"I've got it," he said without preamble. "Let's make the trade."

"Agreed," the metallic voice said, Mandy's captor having apparently gone back to the voice changer now that they were on a landline.

"Where should I meet you?" Parker looked

out the front window, but still couldn't see the two men. "Are you coming here?"

"Go outside and get in the car." As if on cue, the two men pulled up in front of Parker's town house. "My associates will bring you to me."

"Okay." He didn't bother asking why he'd been forced to make the side trip to his apartment—no doubt it had given Mandy's captors time to see that nothing had changed at the Chinatown station, time to make sure the coast was still clear.

"You have sixty seconds to be outside on the sidewalk. No funny stuff." The line went dead.

Outside, the sedan was double parked by the curb. One of the men waited in the driver's seat, the other stood near the rear door, his posture one of casual menace.

Previously Parker had only caught glimpses of the men, and had marked them by their postures and clothing—a tall, slouching man with a black knit cap and thigh-length leather coat, and a shorter, stockier bearded guy wearing a short, thickly lined leather jacket that made him look even stockier.

When Parker reached them and got an up-close look, he saw that both of them wore identical expressions of detached calm that indicated the men were professional hard-asses.

Well, Parker thought, *so am I.* "You my chauffeurs?" he demanded.

"Shut up." The taller man, who was standing outside the car while his buddy waited with his foot on the gas, gave Parker a quick, efficient pat down. He pulled out the minidisk, looked at it and returned it to Parker's jacket. When he found the 9 mm in his waistband, he pulled the gun and held it with easy familiarity. Then he opened the rear door of the sedan. "Get in."

Which meant they didn't just want the data disk, because they could've taken it then and there. For some reason they wanted him, too. Or else they actually were planning on giving him Mandy, unharmed.

He wasn't betting on the latter, but he did feel a spurt of optimism that the search had missed finding the inner pocket with the second evidence envelope.

Come on, Stankowski, he urged. *Use your smarts.*

Parker climbed into the rear of the sedan,

forcing outward impassivity even though his mind was churning. The windows in the rear of the car were heavily tinted, but that didn't worry him because it wasn't as though he wanted to attract attention. He needed to reach Mandy first, and for that, he was on his own.

He had to assume that the two men were in contact with the man holding her, had to assume that they were supposed to call in at regular intervals. That, and the lack of amateur jitters in his captors, meant he would have to time any planned attack perfectly. Too early and the man holding Mandy would know something was wrong. Too late and he'd miss his chance.

Perhaps he already had.

The tall guy got in beside him, still holding the 9 mm, and said, "Drive."

As the vehicle pulled out into unusually sparse traffic, Parker looked out the window, away from the tall man, trying to pretend he was just as tough, just as experienced as they were. For the first time in a long, long time he was grateful for his upbringing, grateful that he'd spent more time on the streets than at the polo club, because he knew he was better off projecting an attitude of "don't waste my time." Fear would only escalate the situation, as would aggression.

"Hey, Radcliff," the tall guy said unexpectedly as the driver turned away from Boston Common.

Parker turned to answer, and got a fist in the face.

Pain exploded and he jerked back, just getting his arms up in time to deflect a second punch, this one from the hand holding his pistol. The blow sang up his arm and sent him reeling back against the far door. Cursing, realizing he'd seriously misread the situation, he got a knee up and used it to hold the tall man off. He threw a punch and felt the impact sing up his knuckles. Shifting, he tried to get leverage, tried to figure out what the hell was going on. He blocked one punch but the next one got through.

The 9 mm connected with his temple, pain exploded in his head, and everything went black.

"EXCELLENT," Deighton said into the disposable phone. "And don't worry about hitting him too hard. It doesn't much matter if he's dead or alive at this point. His body will do."

Parker! Mandy thought, heart going still in her chest. He was talking about Parker. The thugs had hurt him, maybe even killed him. Oh God. What was she going to do?

Rescue seemed an impossibility now.

The politician—still looking shiny and polished and TV ready in his suit and tie—glanced at her. "Durst was an idiot of a genius, but he did get one thing right. Why serve just one purpose when you can multitask?"

With that, he crossed the room and opened the door to the bathroom. The smell of gasoline prickled on the air even before he reached down and grabbed a red plastic five-gallon jug.

Mandy nearly drove the now-bent nail at the end of the wooden slat into her wrist at the sight, and the sudden surge of fear. She forced herself to keep going, though, to keep working on the strands of the nylon rope a little bit at a time. She was making progress, but it was slow going. Too slow, she feared.

Tears ran down her cheeks and her heart felt as though it was breaking in her chest. She sucked in a sobbing breath and kept working at her bonds, though, as Deighton shut the bathroom door, then crossed in front of her to open the window in the main room, letting in a gust of arctic winter air.

The slap of cold biting through her clothing made Mandy flinch, and for a second, her blood-slicked fingers slipped on the wooden slat. It banged against the wall, making a hollow, echoing sound.

Deighton spun and was starting toward her when his phone rang. It was a different ring than before, though, and instead of answering the cheap disposable, he cursed and pulled a slick, expensive phone from the inner pocket of his navy suit jacket.

He checked the caller ID, muttered something under his breath and answered it, sounding suddenly polished and urbane when he said, "Senator, what a coincidence. I was just about to call you."

He turned away from Mandy and crossed to the window, where he stood and breathed clean air while her head spun from the gasoline fumes.

"Did you get a chance to read over the proposal I sent you? I think it would be an excellent forward-thinking move for that area of the city. Some of those old apartment complexes are just a five-alarm fire waiting to happen."

And if they don't happen on their own, you'll make sure they do, Mandy thought as understanding dawned.

Stankowski had been right—it was about politics. Deighton had identified key areas of the city and set out to make problems he could come in and clean up.

He'd created terror so he could become a savior. *Bastard,* she thought, sniffing back tears and trying to fan the anger instead of the sobs.

"Yes, Senator. Thank you. I'll see you then and there," he said into the phone, then clicked it shut and made a satisfied noise. "Here they are. You'll have your boyfriend back in a minute. What's left of him, anyway."

He left the room, heading through the door opposite the bathroom, into the apartment building hallway. He shut the door at his back, leaving her alone.

Sobbing with fear, with grief, she yanked her wrists apart, praying that the rope was weak enough to break.

It held.

"Come on, come *on!*" she chanted, ignoring the pain as she struggled against the bonds and the nylon strands cut into her wrists. She thought she felt the rope give a little, and sick excitement poured through her alongside the fear.

Hearing footsteps in the hallway, she tugged harder, but the ropes didn't loosen, didn't break, leaving her still bound when Deighton returned with his two enforcers behind him.

Between them, they dragged Parker's limp form.

Mandy couldn't stop the low moan from escaping, couldn't stem the tears that ran down her face.

His head, arms and legs hung limply, and the men supported his entire dead weight, puffing from the exertion as they dragged him into the room and dumped him on the sofa. He landed on his side, facing her. She could see red patches and blood on his face, and there was a deep cut on his lip, but no fresh blood ran from the split.

She couldn't tell if he was breathing.

He's not dead, she told herself, refusing to believe it. *He can't be.*

But deep down inside, she felt the scream building—the same scream she'd made as a little girl, when she and her father had returned from their errands, and she'd stepped inside the front door and slipped in her mother's blood.

"You have the disk?" Deighton asked, barely looking at Parker's body.

"Right here." The taller man handed over an evidence bag with the disk inside.

Mandy stared at the minidisk, thinking of everything that had been put into motion the moment she'd pulled Irene Dulbecco's chart off the rack at the E.R.

Deighton tucked the disk inside his suit jacket, lifted his weapon and calmly shot the tall man between the eyes.

The pistol made a popping noise that seemed too quiet for the act.

As the dead man crumpled to the ground and Mandy screamed behind her gag, the shorter guy shouted and went for his own weapon.

Deighton shot him in the temple before he got the gun from his pocket.

The thud of the second man's body hitting the ground seemed agonizingly loud in the sudden silence of the room, which was broken only by Mandy's whimpers.

"This should give the cops some closure, don't you think?" Deighton said conversationally. "These guys kidnapped you and used that as leverage to force Radcliff to recover the disk. There was a scuffle and the good doctor was mortally wounded. He managed to get off a few shots and kill the kidnappers, but unfortunately, he expired before he was able to free you. And the fire?" He shrugged. "They were obviously planning on torching the place to destroy the evidence."

Mandy barely heard him. Her eyes were fixed on the dead men and she was shaking all over. Her tears had dried and her fear had turned to numb shock, and it didn't seem important anymore that she'd managed to get her hands free. Her feet were still bound to the chair, and Deighton was halfway across the room. Even if she grabbed him, what hope did she have of overpowering him?

It was over. She was dead.

Deighton crossed to where his expensive cashmere coat was draped over one of the kitchen chairs, and withdrew a scarf and a cheap disposable lighter. After flicking the lighter, he used another strip from the roll of duct tape to fasten the thumb trigger in the "on" position, and placed the lighter between two of the sofa cushions, near Parker's battered face.

Then he used the soft material to wipe down the pistol he'd just used to kill two men, and bent and placed the weapon near Parker's body.

The sight of Deighton crouched down like that, so casual he was almost whistling as he set the scene, sent an unexpected wash of fury blazing through Mandy's veins. Before she was aware of the impulse or the decision, she screamed and lunged at him.

The lunge carried her partway across the room, dragging the chair with her. She caught the killer by surprise, slamming into him knee-high. Her blow drove him staggering sideways, and he lost his grip on his gun as he roared and fell, banging his head on the edge of the TV stand.

Heart pounding, vision washed red with anger, she belly-crawled across the floor and reached for the gun.

Deighton cursed and kicked it away, then grabbed her by the back of her shirt, catching some of her long hair and twisting it roughly as he dragged her off the ground. He was reeling slightly and bleeding from a cut over his eye.

"Bitch," he snarled, and drew back a fist to punch her in the face.

Before the blow could land, a blur erupted from the sofa and Deighton went smashing to the side.

Parker! Mandy's heart jolted up into her throat and she gaped as the man she'd almost given up for dead swung into action. He was very clearly not dead. And he was furious.

Battered face set in deadly lines, Parker hammered Deighton with a series of blows that sent the killer staggering across the small apartment. He tripped over the fuel can, which tipped over. Gas spilled onto the floor, adding more of a stink to the air.

Deighton feinted and rolled, avoiding Parker's next attack, and scrambled for the gun, which had skidded beneath the kitchen table when he'd kicked it out of Mandy's reach.

Parker dived in pursuit, shouting, "Get the lighter!"

Mandy twisted around, yanking at the knots securing her ankles to the chair. The ropes resisted stubbornly. She was just about to give up and slither across the floor when she felt them start to give.

Working furiously, fingers trembling with the need to hurry, she untied herself, yanked the gag off and scrambled toward the sofa, only to reel back when flames erupted from the cushions.

"Parker!" she screamed. "We've got to get out of here!"

She turned toward him just as Deighton got his hands on the gun. Face gleaming with feral madness, the killer spun and leveled the weapon at Mandy. "You've ruined *everything!*"

Parker grabbed his arm the moment he fired, and the bullet whizzed past Mandy, who was beyond screaming, nearly frozen in terror. In the corner of the room, flame met gasoline and the walls went up in curling ribbons of fire.

Twisting Deighton's gun arm up behind his back, Parker cursed and yanked viciously, dropping the killer to his knees. He cut his eyes to Mandy. "Get out of here."

She shook her head, somehow finding calm amidst the chaos. "Not without you."

He looked at her for a moment, and she couldn't even begin to interpret what she saw in his eyes. Then he nodded, and clubbed Deighton across the temple with his own gun.

The killer went limp in Parker's grip.

"Come on." Parker started across the room, dragging the unconscious man with him.

Then he froze and lifted the pistol as a new commotion sounded in the hall. "Get behind me."

Mandy complied, though the flames were all around them now and the air was growing hotter by the second, gaining smoke and volume and fear.

New terror bloomed. What if that was the sound of reinforcements? What if—

The apartment door burst inward, and she saw dark-clothed men in face masks and riot gear, led by Detective Stankowski's familiar figure.

"It's about time you got here," Parker groused. He reached into his jacket and pulled out a small evidence bag with one of Durst's GPS transmitters inside. "Guess this thing came in handy after all."

He tossed the transmitter to the detective, then said, "Take this garbage. He's got the minidisk on him." He dragged Deighton's limp form forward and dumped the killer on the floor, between the corpses of his associates. Then he turned to Mandy and held out a hand. "Come on. Let's get out of here. The cops can handle the rest."

As he led her out the door, Deighton regained consciousness and began to curse while the cops handcuffed him and dragged him to his feet. Behind them, Mandy heard shouts from the apartment, and the puff of fire extinguishers. Outside, the wail of a fire engine's siren grew louder as the second wave of responders approached.

Out in the hallway, though, there was relative calm as Mandy and Parker walked out of the burning apartment hand in hand.

Nothing was settled between them, but they were alive. Mandy told herself to be content with that, to be grateful that she at least *had* a future.

That lasted until they reached the street, and suited firefighters hustled them back behind a group of barricades. Moments later, Stankowski reappeared and motioned them over to a cluster of police vehicles.

The detective looked harried. "Can you two wait here for a few minutes? I'll need to go over your statements, but things are getting borderline messy inside. We're trying to get as much evidence out of the room as we can before the fire crews open up with the water, but—"

"Go," Parker said quickly. "We'll be here when you can cut yourself free."

The detective nodded and turned away, but then paused and turned back. He held out a hand to Mandy. "I'm sorry you had to go through all this. I wish we could've gotten him sooner, and spared you this whole experience."

She gripped his hand briefly, and felt a strange sense of letdown at the knowledge that while she might see him again, this was the end of their work together. "Don't be sorry," she said softly. "It's over now."

When the detective was gone, the words *it's over* seemed to linger on the air.

Around them there was chaos as other firefighters and rigs arrived, and a crowd of curious onlookers gathered to point and speculate. Near the cruisers, though, it seemed as though a bubble of quiet cocooned Parker and Mandy.

She turned to him and offered her hand as Stankowski had done to her. "Thank you." She paused. "That seems so incredibly inadequate after all you've done for me this week, but I don't think there are words for how grateful I am."

He didn't take her hand, simply looked at it, looked at her as if not sure what he was seeing. "Don't thank me. I should've packed you on a plane that first day and gotten you the hell out of here."

"I wouldn't have gone." She let her hand fall to her side, feeling a beat of depression at the realization that the walls had gone back up and he'd once again retreated inside himself, to the place she couldn't follow.

Well, she was done trying, wasn't she? If they weren't meant to be—if he couldn't

believe in them enough to make it work—
then she was going to have to be enough of
a grown-up to let it go.

So she smiled even though her heart was
breaking, and said, "Don't look so concerned,
Radcliff. We had a deal, and I stand by my
word. I'll be at work first thing Monday, ready
to do my job for you. Move 'em in and ship 'em
out, right? Well, you can consider me shipped
out as of now. It's time for me to go home."

Even though she knew she was supposed
to wait for the detective, she turned and
walked away from him, headed for the road
beyond the barricade, where several taxis had
paused in the traffic. Stankowski knew where
to find her. So did Parker for that matter, but
she suspected she'd see the detective long
before The Boss came calling for her.

And if that thought was enough to have her
breaking down in tears the moment she got
the taxi door closed and promised the driver
she'd get money for him at her apartment, she
was the only one who knew about it.

PARKER TOOK two steps after her before he
made himself stop and stand, watching her go.

"You're an idiot, you know," Stank said, coming up beside him as the cab turned the corner and was lost from sight.

"I know." Parker said, feeling the grief and guilt weighing him down like a rock pressing on the center of his chest.

"You should go after her."

"No." Parker shook his head. "I can't."

Not yet, anyway. He had things to do first.

Chapter Sixteen

Mandy spent the weekend doing normal things. She hung out with Kim and the Wannabes at Jillian's, and even managed to work up to a flirt with a friend-of-a-friend from Mass General. Her heart wasn't in it, though, just as it wasn't into the idea of rearranging her apartment, finishing the unpacking she'd neglected and forcing some sort of style into the place.

She kept trying to remind herself she was lucky to be alive, but the sentiment rang hollow. She might've escaped one fate but she'd fallen to another, one that she knew better than to succumb to a second time. Heartache.

Her father finally called her back Sunday night, and though they might never be close, she did feel as though the experience with

Durst and Deighton had helped her understand him a bit better. They ended the conversation with vague promises to get together, both of them knowing it wouldn't be anytime soon.

By Monday, though, she'd made her decision. Forget waiting for another year worth of E.R. experience—she was going to pull all the strings she could find to win the Meade Fellowship *this* year, damn it, even if it meant calling on her father.

She was done waiting around for her life to start.

When she called to ask where she could send additional references, though, she got a rude shock.

"I'm sorry, Dr. Sparks, but this year's Meade Fellowship has already been decided. The official announcement will be made later this week." On the phone, the administrator's voice brooked no argument. "Would you like me to roll your application through to the next round?"

"Yes, please," Mandy said faintly, her fingers going numb on the handset as she stood in the hallway outside exam room one.

After the admin had hung up the phone, she pressed the handset to her ear to gain a few moments' worth of peace. She turned her back on the rest of the E.R., trying to ignore the organized chaos of a normal Monday morning.

Well, that was just great. She'd finally decided to jump-start her life, and someone else had already beaten her to this year's fellowship.

"Damn it," she muttered under her breath. Then, remembering her new vow not to wait around for things to happen, but instead to *make* them happen, she dialed information, got another number, and punched it in. "Cedar Sinai central operations," a chipper male voice answered. "How may I direct your call?"

"Dr. Stewart Royal, please." Mandy crossed her fingers, and was rewarded when the operator simply put her through without asking why a lowly E.R. doc would want to speak with the head of the Meade Foundation.

Based on life with her father, she half expected her call to head straight to voice mail. Shock shimmered through her when the line went live and a man's voice said, "Royal here."

"Dr. Royal, this is...this is Mandy, um, Dr. Amanda Sparks from Boston General." She shook her head to clear it, wishing she'd planned out what she wanted to say.

Before she could fumble onward, he said in a cheerful voice, "Of course, Mandy, I'm glad you called. May I be among the first to congratulate you?"

"Huh?"

"On the Meade Fellowship," he said, then paused. "Radcliff hasn't told you yet?"

"No," she said, her voice dropping to a whisper as her throat closed in on itself. "He hasn't told me anything."

"Well then, it's my pleasure to tell you that based on your supervisor's glowing recommendation and supporting documentation from the Boston Police Department, praising your guts and scientific acumen, that you've been awarded this year's Meade Fellowship." He paused, and she could hear the smile in his voice when he said, "You're going to China, Dr. Sparks. Dr. Wong is looking forward to working with you. He'll expect you two weeks from tomorrow."

Mandy leaned her forehead against the

cool tiles of the corridor wall and concentrated on breathing. "Thank you," she finally said. "I'm honored, and I'll do my very best to make the Meade Foundation proud."

"I'm sure you will." Dr. Royal paused, as if expecting her to say something else. When she didn't, he chuckled. "I'm going to hang up now and let you process that information. If you have any questions, please don't hesitate to call."

Mandy whispered, "Thank you," again, her vocabulary having apparently devolved to those two words.

This time when the line went dead, she hung up the phone. Then she turned to face the E.R., staring around and feeling as though she'd never seen the place before. Worse, she was pretty sure she'd never see it again once she left this time.

And she knew that was exactly what Parker intended.

Hurt and angry almost beyond words, even though she was equally elated, she marched past the front desk, ignoring Aimee calling her name, no doubt to remind her that she had patients backing up and it was her job to process them as efficiently as possible.

"I'll show him efficiency," she muttered as she shoved through Parker's office door. "I'm sure you told yourself you were doing me a favor, but—"

She broke off. The office was empty. And not just empty as in there was nobody at the desk. Empty as in there was almost nothing on the desk, or anywhere else, for that matter.

A few boxes were stacked against the wall, neatly labeled in Parker's slanting, masculine script, making it look as though she wasn't the only one leaving.

But that didn't make any sense. He'd gotten what he wanted, hadn't he? She wasn't going to be at Boston General much longer, because whether or not she appreciated his methods or his motivation, she'd gotten the fellowship and was headed for China.

But if that was the case, where was he going?

Refusing to feel even the faintest flicker of hope, she spun on her heel and marched back to the front desk, intending to demand the whereabouts of The Boss.

She didn't need to, though. He was standing by the front desk, talking to Aimee, who was no doubt reporting Mandy's behavior. Little tattletale.

Still fuming, though a little confused, too, Mandy strode across the E.R. lobby and faced Parker. She put her hands on her hips and glared up at him, knowing she was creating just the sort of scene he preferred to avoid and not caring in the slightest. "Am I supposed to thank you?"

Expression as cool as ever—damn him— he looked down at her. "It'd be a nice start."

"Don't hold your breath," she snapped, but then reminded herself that she was a grown-up and a professional. She gestured toward the lounge. "Should we take this somewhere private?"

He just stood there for a beat, then crossed his arms and leaned back against the main desk, seeming, for some reason, amused. "I think not."

His amused indifference only added to her pique. She blew out a breath. "Fine. You want to throw down here? Let's go, *boss.* First off, you wouldn't have hired me if you didn't want to, pressure from above or not, which means either you were testing yourself, or you really didn't care either way about seeing me again. I think we've proven the latter isn't true, so I'm going with the former. Well, guess what? Same thing goes—I wanted to prove to myself that I was over you."

"Did it work?"

"You know damn well it didn't, which is undoubtedly why you called in however many favors it took to get me the Meade Fellowship a year ahead of schedule." Mandy was aware that her tirade had attracted the attention of pretty much the entire E.R., staff and patients alike. She didn't care anymore, though. She stepped up to him, getting in his face when she said, "You've got what you wanted. I'm leaving in two weeks. Hell, I'll leave today if that's what you want. What I don't get are the boxes. Why are you packing?"

There wasn't an ounce of change in his expression, but somehow the air warmed when he said, "Because I'm going with you."

PARKER WATCHED the expressions flicker across her face in rapid succession: shock was followed by suspicion before he saw a flash of something that gave him hope.

"Why?" she said, getting straight to the heart of the matter in typical Mandy fashion.

The answer was something he'd been hoping to work up to, but since she asked he forced himself to answer with the simple truth. "Because I'm not only crazy about you, I love you, and I want to be with you no matter where you are. If that means going to China and learning about plants, then that's what I'll do." He paused, and said quietly. "If you'll have me, that is."

An absolute hush descended, as though the staff members and patients were all holding their breaths, waiting for her answer.

Or maybe it was just him holding his breath. He'd spent the weekend convincing himself that this was the way to go. Stank hadn't been totally on board, but Parker told himself that he knew Mandy better, that she'd appreciate the spontaneity from him. But as she just stood there, looking at him, he suddenly realized she could take it exactly the opposite, that he was being controlling rather than spontaneous, that he'd just made the biggest decision of their relationship without talking to her first.

Fear tightened his gut. Had he blown it at the most crucial moment?

"Look, Mandy," he began, feeling the first prickles of flop sweat and mentally scrambling for a way to backpedal before she turned him down flat. "I don't want you to think that I'm making decisions for you. Think of this as a request. Hell, I'll beg if you want me to. Let me come with you. Give us a chance to—"

She launched herself at him, cutting him off midword as she wrapped her arms around his neck and cut him off with a hard, smacking kiss.

The slippery, coiled knots that had tied him up all weekend—hell, ever since she'd come back into his life—loosened all at once and he brought his arms up to hold her, hard, as she twined herself around him. Laughing, he kissed her back, and kept on kissing her even through a smattering of applause and a chorus of wolf whistles from the crowd.

To hell with decorum. He wasn't letting this one walk out of his life. Not ever again.

AFTER A KISS that was both too long for a public place and too short for Mandy's taste, she pulled away and looked up at him, finally seeing the emotion in his eyes. The love. "I love you back."

"China?" he said, as though everything else was already settled between them.

"Are you sure? You don't even believe in homeopathy."

He shrugged, a rueful grin tugging at his lips. "Who knows? Maybe I'll learn something new."

"I think I can guarantee that." She stepped away from him, pressed a hand against her jittering stomach and exhaled. "Whew. I can't catch my breath."

"I know the feeling." He caught her hand and twined their fingers together. "Care to adjourn to my office so we can make some plans?"

Mandy's heart lifted as she finally began to realize—and believe—that the impossible had become possible, that she could have the man she loved, that he could love her back. Only a few days earlier she'd been close to dying.

Now, the future spread out in front of her, bright and shining with potential.

She smiled. "You're The Boss."

He grinned crookedly. "I think from now on we can share that responsibility. That's what families do, right?"

As proposals went it wasn't much, Mandy thought. Yet, coming from Parker, it was exactly right.

"Yes," she said, taking his hand as the E.R. erupted with applause and cheers. "That's what families do."

* * * * *

In 2008 look for more stories of gripping romantic suspense from reader favorite Jessica Andersen, only from Harlequin Intrigue!

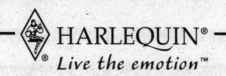

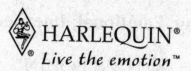

HARLEQUIN®

SuperRomance®

...there's more to the story!

Superromance.
A *big* satisfying read about unforgettable
characters. Each month we offer *six* very different
stories that range from family drama to adventure
and mystery, from highly emotional stories to
romantic comedies—and much more! Stories
about people you'll believe in and care about.
Stories too compelling to put down....

Our authors are among today's *best* romance
writers. You'll find familiar names and talented
newcomers. Many of them are award winners—
and you'll see why!

If you want the biggest and best
in romance fiction, you'll get it
from Superromance!

Exciting, Emotional, Unexpected...

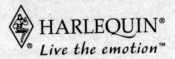

HARLEQUIN®
Live the emotion™

HARLEQUIN®
Presents

The world's bestselling romance series...
The series that brings you your favorite authors,
month after month:

Helen Bianchin...Emma Darcy
Lynne Graham...Penny Jordan
Miranda Lee...Sandra Marton
Anne Mather...Carole Mortimer
Susan Napier...Michelle Reid

and many more uniquely talented authors!

Wealthy, powerful, gorgeous men...
Women who have feelings just like your own...
The stories you love, set in exotic, glamorous locations...

HARLEQUIN®
Presents

Seduction and Passion Guaranteed!

Harlequin® Historical
Historical Romantic Adventure!

Imagine a time of chivalrous knights and unconventional ladies, roguish rakes and impetuous heiresses, rugged cowboys and spirited frontierswomen— these rich and vivid tales will capture your imagination!

Harlequin Historical . . . they're too good to miss!

SPECIAL EDITION™

Emotional, compelling stories that capture the intensity of living, loving and creating a family in today's world.

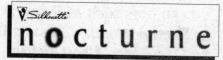

Modern, passionate reads that are powerful and provocative.

Dramatic and sensual tales of paranormal romance.

Romantic SUSPENSE

Romances that are sparked by danger and fueled by passion.

SDIR07

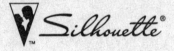